BUMMER
SUMMER

BUMMER SUMMER

by Ann M. Martin

AN
APPLE
PAPERBACK

SCHOLASTIC INC.
New York Toronto London Auckland Sydney

ISBN 0-590-41308-2

12 11 10 9 8 7 6 5 4 3 2 1   7 8 9/8 0/9

Printed in the U.S.A.   11

For Granny, my favorite critic, with love.
And for Louise Colligan. Thank you.

Contents

CHAPTER 1

The Wedding

The thing I'll always remember about the wedding is blue hair. That was the color Mrs. Samuels had dyed hers the week before. I swear it. Blue. I was standing facing Dr. Haber, our minister, in one of those church-in-the-round places where the pews are built in a circle around the altar so everybody can see what is going on. Mrs. Samuels was just a few pews behind Dr. Haber, trying to see over his left shoulder. Since I was told to hold still during the ceremony, I had nothing to do but stare at her new blue hair for thirty minutes.

Believe it or not, I was the maid of honor at my father's wedding. No kidding. Not too many kids get to do that. Be at their own father's wedding, I mean. But there I was, twelve years old, dressed in a hideous long pink flowered gown (when you're in a wedding, you wear a *gown,* not a dress—that was one of the important things I learned from my step-grandmother-to-be), and carrying a pink and white *floral bouquet* (another wedding term, meaning bunch of flowers), which I was very allergic to.

My father was marrying Kate, who was going to be my stepmother. Yesterday she'd been Kate Parker. Today she would be Kate Whitlock. *Kate Whitlock.* I tossed the name around in my head while my uncle, who

3

was the best man, read a poem about peace and joy and everlasting love.

Kate Whitlock. It sounded O.K. Not as good as Annie Whitlock, though. That had been my mother's name. She died when I was four.

I never thought my father would remarry. He and I had been fine—just the two of us—with Mrs. Meade, our housekeeper. I thought we were very happy. But last fall Dad met Kate and that was that. You know how those things go. They liked each other, then they loved each other, then they decided to get married, and here we all were, in church.

Except it wasn't that easy. Kate wasn't unattached. She was a package deal. You got her, and you got Muffin and Baby Boy, too. Muffin was her three-year-old daughter. Her real name was Melissa. Heaven knows how Kate got "Muffin" out of that. And Baby Boy was her two-month-old unnamed son. (I called him Baby Boy because his hospital bracelet said Baby Boy Parker, and Kate hadn't come up with a name for him yet. I suggested Joshua about a million times but nobody paid any attention.) We were going to be a great family, because my name is kind of weird, too. I am Kammy, short for Kamilla, which is a name that's been in my mother's family forever. Dad and Kate, Muffin, Baby Boy, and Kammy. Splendid.

Anyway, Kate was pregnant with Baby Boy when her husband picked up and left her last summer. Just like that. No note or anything. One day he was there, the next day he was gone. Several weeks later Kate met my father, and the rest is history.

Someone in the congregation was reading another

poem. I never knew Dad and Kate liked poetry so much.

About ten minutes into the ceremony my eyes began to blur from staring at Mrs. Samuels's blue hair. I wished I didn't have to hold quite so still. Muffin was the flower girl and she was standing next to me. She'd been told to hold still, too, but so far she'd been craning her neck all over the place, standing on one foot and scratching her ankle with the other, patting her hair, and sniffing her basket of flower petals. (Floral petals?) At least she wasn't crying, which was what she had been doing loudly and nonstop for about an hour before the ceremony. She was such a pain. I could not believe she'd be moving into my house in a week.

Pain or not, I had to admit Muffin was adorable. She was a storybook girl with soft blond hair, sparkly blue eyes, and a cherubic dimpled smile that she'd give to anybody whenever she wanted something. She gave it to the lady behind the candy counter at Bamberger's last Tuesday and got a free root beer drop. (I smiled at the lady and got my change.)

For the wedding, Muffin was wearing short white socks, black patent leather Mary Janes, and a yellow checked dress with a white apron that had daisies on it. You should have seen what we went through getting that dress. We went to the Quakerbridge Mall, and after two hours of fussing and complaining from one end of Saks's children's department to the other, Muffin finally liked a dress. (I didn't know a three-year-old could tell a dress from a diaper.) Unfortunately, the only one in her size had no daisies on the apron. When the salesman said they'd order one in her size with daisies, but it would take a week, Muffin burst into real tears, complete with

a fire engine wail, which set off Baby Boy in his Snugli
carrier. (This was the main reason I was wearing the
ghastly pink gown. We found it in five minutes, it fit, and
we were able to buy it and get it out of Saks before
Muffin was arrested for disturbing the peace.)

Luckily we didn't have to buy anything for Baby Boy
to wear to the wedding. He'd been christened the Sunday before, so he just wore his christening outfit again.
Kate said probably no one would notice. I said I didn't
think anyone would care even if they did notice. Dad
said that was not a nice thing to say.

By shifting my eyes very slightly to the left I could see
Baby Boy in the congregation. He was on the lap of
Kate's mother (the Wedding Queen) and he was sound
asleep. I guessed that was O.K. As long as he wasn't
squawking. Last week when the minister put the water
on his head, he arched his back and shrieked so loudly he
practically caved the church in. Kate's face got very red.
I had been glad I was sitting in the back.

Suddenly I noticed the church was quiet. Everyone
was seated expectantly on the red-cushioned pews. Dad
and Kate were standing very solemnly. That meant the
poetry readings and all the weird stuff were over. The
real wedding part could begin.

Of course, all the dumb parts were Kate's. She gets
some very strange ideas, and Dad always seems to give
in to them. Like the time last month when Kate decided
we needed some exercise. I thought, fine, we'll all take a
little walk, and Muffin can ride her tricycle. But no, Kate
had *roller skating* in mind—for everyone, including
Muffin and Dad. We went to this sports store in town
where you can rent the good kind of skates, and we took

them to a road behind our house where there is very little traffic.

Dad and Muffin were terrible. Kate was pretty good, and I go skating a lot, so I was O.K., too. But I didn't have any fun. It was embarrassing to watch my father edging along the curb, grabbing out for Kate or trees or anything, and falling down every few feet, but laughing the entire time. All I can say is it's a good thing we were on that unused road, because we live in one of those tiny New England towns where everybody knows everybody, and if any of my friends had seen us, I would have been mortified.

It was things like the roller skating that made me hate Kate. Really. She was impossible. For the last six months she and Dad had spent every second of their spare time together. I never got to see Dad by himself anymore. Kate was always hogging him. Plus, every other sentence out of Dad's mouth began with "Kate says." "Kate says we shouldn't eat so much red meat." "Kate says you don't get enough sleep." Couldn't he think for himself anymore? I was so sick of it I could have killed her. And Kate always tried to sic Muffin on me. Actually, I think she just wanted Muffin and me to be friends, but as I've mentioned, Muffin was a three-year-old pain. Besides, Muffin was so busy trying to wrap my father around her chubby little finger that she hardly had time for me. Then there was Baby Boy. Before he was born, Kate had tried being really palsy-walsy and friendly with me, always bringing me little gifts—barrettes and earrings and stuff—but I wouldn't fall for that. Because then Baby Boy came and she changed, just like I knew she would. After all, he and Muffin were her real children, but who was I? I was almost glad when she stopped paying so much attention to me.

The silence in the church was broken by a resounding organ chord. It made Muffin jump. I saw her screw up her face, and for one horrifying moment I thought she was going to cry right in the middle of everything. Then she looked up at me and I gave her a little smile to let her know it was O.K. She gritted her teeth and smiled back. At that moment, as much as she annoyed me, I felt kind of proud of Muffin. She was trying very hard to be good.

The organ struck a softer chord and launched into "Amazing Grace." Everyone stood up and began singing. I knew parts of the hymn, so I sang along when I could, but I didn't have a hymn book. From over Dr. Haber's shoulder I could hear the lady with the blue hair. She sang in one of those high, wavery, extremely loud voices, but she wasn't *quite* on key. That really bothered me because I like to sing and I happen to have perfect pitch. It was my turn to grit my teeth.

I tried not to look at Mrs. Samuels. Instead I glanced over at Dad. I thought about how he and my real mother must have stood at the front of a church once. That would have been three years before I was born. I wondered what my father looked like then. Now he had thick, curly hair, a tickly mustache, and laughing brown eyes. Probably he looked the same fifteen years ago but with no gray hairs. (I would give anything to have wavy hair like Dad's. But no, mine is straight and fine like my mother's, and the same honey color. That's one of the few things I remember about her.)

Kate must have stood in front of an altar another time, too. Maybe five or six years ago. She would have been about twenty then. Pretty young. She is nineteen whole years younger than my father. She could be his daughter, for heaven's sake.

I remembered the first time I met Kate and Muffin. It was last Thanksgiving. Dad and I always did something special and different at Thanksgiving. Once we went to Williamsburg, Virginia, for a colonial meal. Another time we spent four days at Disney World. I looked forward to planning a new trip for the two of us every year. But last year Dad didn't say anything about the holiday until sometime after Halloween—long after we usually started planning. When he suggested that we "just stay at home," I knew something was up.

I was wondering if we could invite anyone over for the meal, like maybe our cousins in Trumbull, and he said slowly, "Yes, I did think someone might share dinner with us, but the people I had in mind are fairly new in town. You haven't met them yet. They're Mrs. Parker, a biology professor at the university, and her little girl. Melissa is three, I believe."

"That's *all?*" I asked. "Just *two* people, one of them possibly in training pants?"

"Well, there's a little more," he said. "You see, Kate—Mrs. Parker, that is—and I have been spending some time together recently."

No joke, I thought to myself. You think I didn't notice how little you've been around the last month or so?

"Her husband left her recently," Dad went on, "and she's been lonely. We've gotten to know each other quite well, and I'd like you to get to know her, too. I thought Thanksgiving dinner would be an ideal time for everyone to get acquainted."

There was an uncomfortable silence.

Finally I said, "I don't think I really have a say, do I? You've already made the plans, right?"

"Well, I—"

"Forget it," I sputtered. "Sure, sure, dinner with the Parkers is great." I stormed out of the room then, with big plans for cutting out on the meal. Maybe my cousins would invite me to their house. Or I'd hurt myself the night before and land in the hospital instead. But underneath it all I knew I'd be there, and somehow I also knew my life would not be the same afterward.

On Thanksgiving Day, Dad and I were busy all morning. Once I got used to the idea of who was coming for dinner, the preparations were fun. Sort of.

Mrs. Meade, who would be spending the holiday with her sister's family, had cooked up a storm for us the two days before Thanksgiving. She made two pies, one kind I hated (pumpkin) and one kind I loved (apple cinnamon), and let me help with the crust. She also concocted all these vegetable dishes. She never used recipes. She just walked around the kitchen grabbing carrots and onions and parsley and turnips, and chopping and peeling and boiling and frying. All very calmly. Neatly, too.

Anyway, by Thanksgiving morning, the dishes were carefully labeled and stored in the freezer and refrigerator. The only things Dad and I had to do were defrost the stuff, set the table, and, of course, handle the turkey. This was not so easy.

The night before, Dad had said to me, "I'll get up at five to start the bird." (He always calls chickens and turkeys "birds.") "Don't you worry about a thing, pumpkin. Just get up when you feel like it." I said O.K., but giggled to myself, knowing what would happen.

At five o'clock I heard Dad's alarm go off. It sounded like a factory whistle. Sometimes I sleep through it; sometimes I don't. That morning I didn't. I woke up with butterflies in my stomach. Not just a few. A whole flock.

Then I heard a thump and Dad hissed, "Darn it." He may have broken another toe. He breaks about a toe a year stubbing them on things. He is not the world's most coordinated person. I heard him fumble his way into the bathroom and later fumble his way downstairs. I knew that behind him would be a trail of stuff he had dropped or tripped over.

So I got up and followed the trail downstairs. It consisted of a hand towel, a sock, a Kleenex, his glasses, and an overturned wastebasket. I picked up the glasses and brought them to him in the kitchen. He was staring into the oven, looking confused.

"Dad?" I said. "Good morning. Happy Thanksgiving."

He looked around sleepily. "Morning, sweetie."

"Here are your glasses," I said, holding them out to him. "What are you doing?"

"Trying to remember the temperature." He put his glasses on.

"The temperature to set the oven to? Wait, here are Mrs. Meade's instructions." I pulled an index card out of his bathrobe pocket.

"Oh, good . . . good girl," he mumbled.

We got the turkey all straightened out, and Dad went back to bed for a couple of hours. I fixed breakfast for us. It's my best meal. I'm a whiz with a toaster.

Around eight-thirty Dad came to life. By eleven o'-
clock we were ready to start setting the table.

"O.K., Kams," he said with relish, "what do you think?
The white linen tablecloth or the green holiday damask?"

What? You're giving *me* a *choice?* Does it matter what
I want? "How about the green damask?" I asked slowly,
watching him out of the corners of my eyes. He loves the
white linen.

"Okey-doke," he said. Not a glimmer of hesitation.

We bustled around, getting out all the stuff we never
use—butter dishes, silver, pie servers, creamers.

"Time for the finishing touches," Dad announced, just
when I thought the table was really ready. "Let's go
upstairs and I'll show you something."

We trooped up to the third floor, Dad leading the way.
When we reached the end of the hall, I stood and looked
out the little round window there, while Dad fiddled
with the pole and ceiling ring for the attic stairs. It's my
own private window. I happen to know that if you stand
exactly four inches from the glass and narrow your eyes
properly, the oak limb outside turns into a reaching
hand. And if the wind blows just right, the fingers
beckon you to . . .

"Oof. Here we go." Dad had pulled the trap door
down and unfolded the stairs.

We climbed up.

Ordinarily I am not allowed in the attic because the
floor isn't finished and Dad says if I step on the wrong
spot I will fall through the ceiling and land in the third
floor bathroom. I do not know if this is true, but I don't
care to test it.

Dad came to a sudden halt at the top of the stairs and

I ran into him, almost causing him to break another toe.

"Here," he said. "This box."

I peered around him and could just make out the words printed on top of a large cardboard carton: TABLE —HOLIDAY.

Dad stepped on into the attic. I hoped he knew where the unfinished places were.

"I'll just sit here on the top step," I said as he settled himself on that dangerous floor.

Dad smiled at me and opened the box. Mostly it looked like wads of tissue paper inside.

"Your mother was a great organizer," he said quietly, unwrapping a white bundle. For a few seconds he just kept unwinding layers. He was far away. "We haven't used this stuff much. I don't think you'll remember seeing it, but you have. All of it." He carefully placed the tissue paper in the box and held something out to me.

It was a flat piece of china—a little white rectangle with yellow and pink roses around the border, but nothing in the middle.

"What is it?" I had to ask.

"It's a place card, sweetie. See, you write in your guest's name with water colors. Then you can wash it off later."

"Oh, what a neat idea!" I cried. "Are there more?"

"There should be sixteen."

"What else is in here?" I asked, pawing carefully through the little white mounds.

"Lots of things," said Dad. "All the fancy things for holidays. We used the place cards at every holiday meal —Easter, Thanksgiving, Christmas. One year we used them for your birthday."

"My birthday?"

"Yes. Your mother threw a huge party when you turned four."

I was surprised. I didn't remember ever having a birthday party. That was not how Dad and I did things. We would spend the day at the beach (my birthday is at the end of August), or go to the state park, or see a movie. Then we'd go home to a special dinner prepared by Mrs. Meade (menu chosen by me), and I'd open my cards and gifts, and then we'd talk a little while and go to bed. It was lots of fun and very special. But I did not recall a single actual party.

"Why did my mother give me a big party when I was four? Did I have a party every year? Did Mother like parties?"

"Slow down!" said Dad, smiling gently, and adjusting his glasses. "Let's see. Well, your mother . . . your mother was very social. She and I could not have been more different in that respect. Why she ever chose *me*, a stuffy old economics professor, I'll never know."

"Oh, *Dad*," I said. "You weren't old then. And you are not stuffy," I added quickly.

"Well. At any rate, she was pretty, Kams, very pretty. You know the photo of her that sits on the piano? That was taken when she was nineteen. She had a lovely, soft face, and hair like sunlight, and an easy laugh. That was one thing I liked best about her. She laughed whenever something struck her funny. She never held back." Dad sighed. "Anyway, she looked just as pretty when she was twenty, and when she was twenty-five, and when she was twenty-seven and died."

"Were you sad then?" I asked suddenly, without really thinking.

"When? When she died?"

I nodded.

"Yes," he said slowly. "I was very sad. I couldn't even take care of you for a while. I sent you to live with your uncle Paul and aunt Adele for a couple of months. Do you remember that?"

"No." I shook my head.

"And then I hired Mrs. Meade to help us out. I just couldn't do everything myself."

"That's O.K., Dad."

Dad patted my hand absent-mindedly. He was answering my questions, but I got the distinct impression he was talking to himself.

"Anyway, your mother liked nothing better than a lot of excitement, a big whirl of fun and people. Before we got married she lived in Boston, and I bet she was the most popular girl there. A debutante, parties every weekend. And after we were married and moved here, she picked up where she left off, except she was the hostess, not the guest, at all the parties.

"For every holiday, every occasion, your mother could be counted on to have a terrific party. Our friends and relatives looked forward to them. Annie would spend weeks going over menus, planning the table, inviting guests." He broke off. "Yes. She was special."

"What about my birthday, Dad?" At times like this, when we're talking and sharing ourselves, I want to call my father "Daddy" again, like I did when I was little, but I never do. I do not want to sound childish.

"Oh, yes. Your fourth birthday! It wasn't a children's party like most four-year-olds would have, with pin-the-tail-on-the-donkey, and relay races, and a puppet show.

Instead it was a huge dinner party. It was on a Sunday, I remember. Your grandparents came, all four of them, and lots of cousins and aunts and uncles, and neighbors with their children. It was a real event. And after the cocktails and the present-opening, most people sort of drifted away, until just the grandparents and a few close friends were left. They had all been invited for dinner.

"I remember Annie, your mother, saying to you, 'You're the guest of honor, Mouse, so you sit at the head of the table and wear the crown.' Do you remember that she called you Mouse?"

I shook my head. I wished I did, though.

"And she had a real tiara for you, not a paper crown. She would have made your childhood a fairy tale, if she could.

"Annie and I sat next to each other at the opposite end of the table. She held my hand and smiled at me when the cake came, just as if she were the birthday girl. The party was as much fun for her as it was for you.

"And that was our last big to-do. The car accident was just about two weeks later. Right after the funeral I went through the cupboards and chests in the dining room and moved all this party stuff upstairs. It was so much your mother, I just couldn't have it around."

"But Dad, do you think," I asked earnestly, "do you think we could use it today? Maybe not all of it, but a little of it?"

"I kind of thought we should," he said. "It's a real party at last."

"We've had other parties," I said suspiciously.

"But no fancy ones. Just pizza parties or barbecues or eggnog get-togethers. This one is different. I'd like it to be special."

I decided it would be dangerous to pursue the subject, even though Dad was quiet, waiting for me to speak.

I unwrapped another package.

"I hope you have a good time today, Kammy." Dad paused. "I want you to like Kate and her daughter." He was twisting his handkerchief so tightly, the top of his index finger had turned bright red. "I like Kate a lot and I—"

"Napkin rings!" I interrupted him. I was still exploring the contents of the box, and the tissue paper had revealed a china ring with a rose pattern matching the place cards. "Ooh, can we use these, too?" I asked.

"Of course," said Dad. "Find the others. Or better yet, let's just bring the box downstairs. We'll probably need these things from time to time now."

"O.K." I put the unwrapped pieces carefully on top of the box. But I didn't get up. Dad and I just looked at each other. Finally I said, "This is nice stuff."

Dad moved over next to me and put his arms around me. "Yeah. Nice stuff."

I hugged him as hard as I could.

Mrs. Parker and Melissa (that's what I called them then) showed up near noon on Thanksgiving. Right away I had three shocks. When Mrs. Parker handed her coat to my father and turned to face me, I saw that she was *pregnant*. For sure. No joke. I mean, you could tell. She wasn't fat anywhere except one place, and she was wearing a very loose jumper with no belt or tie.

The next two shocks came during the introductions. Mrs. Parker held out her hand and said to me, "I'm Mrs. Parker. Please call me Kate. And this is Melissa. Everyone calls her Muffin."

Muffin? She was the first person I had ever met who

was named after a breakfast food.

And *Kate*. In some ways that was worse. I am not
allowed to call anyone over twenty-one by his or her first
name unless the person's a relative. This is a hard-and-
fast rule. Breaking it meant one of three things. Kate was
under twenty-one. (False.) She was a distant relative.
(Probably also false.) She was going to become very close
to our family. (I hoped that was false, but I had my
doubts.)

My father stopped a deadly silence by saying brightly,
"Well, why don't we all sit down?"

So we trooped into the living room, where I'd put out
these bowls of salted nuts and this plate of cheese slices
and Ritz crackers.

Dad and Kate immediately squeezed themselves into
our antique green velvet love seat, and Muffin pounced
on the miniature rocking chair that Dad had made me
drag out of the attic that morning. My old chair.

I dumped myself on the far end of the couch and
surveyed things. Four people in their good holiday
clothes, sitting in the spacious living room of an old
colonial home, with an early snow falling outside the bay
windows. Except for me, it would have been a nice family scene. Mr. and Mrs. America and their perfect little
child.

Kate was truly beautiful, even if she was pregnant. In
fact, she was just a bigger version of Muffin, with rosy
coloring and blond (almost white) hair, which she coiled
up on her head. She was very tall, I had noticed, and
sitting down, she and Dad looked just the same height.
What a couple. . . . Couple.

The day went fairly well. Muffin and I went up to my

room and watched the Macy's Thanksgiving Parade on TV. Muffin was sweet. She giggled a lot, but she didn't say much.

Dinner was all right, too. At least until near the end. Kate had been asking me all these dumb questions, like did I enjoy school, did I play sports, did I have a best friend? I was sitting across the table from her, and suddenly, as I listened to her talk and watched her cut Muffin's turkey and mash up her carrots, I found I wasn't seeing Kate at all. I was seeing my own mother, my pretty blond mother cutting my food and asking me about nursery school.

"Excuse me," I said quickly and dashed into the kitchen. I stood there for a minute resting my forehead against the cool refrigerator. Then I splashed some water on my dress like I had to get out a spot or something, and walked bravely back into the dining room.

Just as I got to my place at the table, Muffin knocked over her milk.

"Oh, Melissa," sighed her mother.

It must have been really important that Kate called her Melissa, because Muffin started to cry.

I waited patiently for someone to ask her to apologize or give her a napkin so she could mop up. It was, after all, our good damask tablecloth that was getting stained, and Dad and Mrs. Meade had always taught me to be responsible for whatever I did. It was an unspoken rule. If you break something, you fix it; if you tear something, you sew it; and if you spill something, you clean it up.

So I was more than a little surprised when my father said sharply, "Kammy, for heaven's sake, go get the paper towels."

I felt like he'd hit me. I stumbled into the kitchen, grabbed the paper towels, and slammed the cabinet door shut. Then I flounced into the dining room and jabbed away at the wet place. No one even paid attention. Both Dad and Kate were fawning over Muffin as if they'd just paid the ransom and gotten her back from kidnapers. It was only *milk*, for pete's sake.

Dinner ended after I'd finished mopping up the table and Kate finished mopping up Muffin's face. She held a hiccupping Muffin in her lap and said, "Robert, this has been so nice. Really. We've enjoyed ourselves very much, haven't we, baby?" For one horrifying moment I thought she was referring to my *father*, but she meant Muffin.

Muffin gave one final hiccup and stuck her thumb in her mouth.

"I think Muffin's ready for a nap," said Kate. "Let me help you clear up, and then we'd better be on our way."

"Oh, that's not necessary. Kammy and I will clean up later. Muffin looks pooped."

Ten minutes later we stood at the front door saying our good-byes.

"It was certainly nice to meet you, Kammy." Kate smiled. "I'm glad I finally had the chance."

"Me, too," I lied, speaking directly to my feet.

Kate took Muffin's hand and whispered, "What do you say, honey?"

"Thank you," she mumbled to no one in particular. She looked straight into my father's eyes and produced her famous smile. I thought Dad might actually *cry*.

Then Dad drew Kate to him and kissed her. On the mouth. It wasn't one of those long goopy kisses like in the movies, but it was no quick peck either.

They hugged briefly, and I just stared. Finally Dad walked them out to their car. When he came back in I was standing where he had left me, my head bowed.

He lifted my chin so I had to look at him. "What did you think?" he asked gently.

"About what? Mrs. Parker and Melissa? They're O.K."

"You can call them Kate and Muffin, Kams."

I'd been calling them those names in my head, but it was harder to say them out loud. "Why? Why can I call her Kate?" I asked. "She's over twenty-one, and I bet she's not a relative."

"Because she's very special to me, sweetheart. *Very* special. I tried to tell you that bef—"

I pulled away from Dad, turned and walked into the kitchen. It was cleanup time.

"You may kiss the bride."

I looked up, startled. I had dreamed my way right through the exchange of rings and everything.

Dad and Kate were in each other's arms. Then they turned around, grinning broadly. I once heard someone say something about a radiant bride. Well, that was Kate. Radiant.

Muffin ran over to them, uncertain about what she was supposed to do, even though we had been through all that several times at the rehearsal last night. What she ended up doing now was disgusting. We had decided that she would walk out of the church in front of Dad and Kate, strewing petals all down the aisle. Instead she put her basket over one arm and, smiling adorably, held out her hands to Dad and Kate. They each took one, and the three of them walked out of the church together,

Muffin in the middle. I could have strangled her. Everyone, of course, thought she was charming. The lady with
the blue hair started to cry.

My uncle took my arm, and we walked out behind the
Three Musketeers. I don't think anybody except Uncle
Paul even looked at me. I could have been wearing a rain
barrel.

Dad and Kate stepped outside, let go of Muffin, who
was taken over by the Wedding Queen, and stepped
right into a waiting car. It was covered with shaving
cream and crepe paper and had a bunch of tin cans tied
to the back. A large, tacky sign on the hood said JUST
MARRIED (no kidding, I thought) and an ugly Kewpie doll
bride was stuck on the radio antenna.

My father and Kate waved to us all through the front
window and drove off. There wasn't going to be a wedding reception. There weren't any good-byes either. Not
even for Muffin and me.

They just drove off. They were headed for their honeymoon in Puerto Rico. The lucky stiffs.

Muffin started to cry.

I waited until I got to the ladies' room before I did, too.

CHAPTER 2

Moving Day

Exactly one week after the wedding I was sitting alone on the front stoop of our house. It was a perfect June day. Our yard was green and shady and smelled good. Ordinarily I'd have been sitting on the lawn, except that it was caterpillar season. I don't mind the caterpillars but I hate the webs they spin when they swing around in the trees. You can never be sure you're not walking into a spider's web.

So today was the day. I was waiting. Just waiting. Mrs. Meade was the only other person at home. Our house was cool and dark and big and empty-feeling. I should have been inside enjoying all the emptiness because it wasn't going to last much longer, but the weather was too beautiful to miss. Besides, Simon, my new orangey-tan kitten, was sound asleep in my lap, all his little legs and his tail in a big bunch. I didn't want to disturb him, so I sat.

And waited.

They'd be arriving any minute. Kate, Muffin, and Baby Boy. It was moving-in day. Dad had rented a U-Haul and driven it over to their apartment early in the morning. While he was gone I was supposed to be doing some stuff to the room that would be Muffin's and Baby Boy's, but I just couldn't. It was too hard. It had been our special guest bedroom with yellow flowered wallpaper, the old canopy bed, and the window seat with cushions that matched the wallpaper.

But not anymore. The furniture had been moved to a room on the third floor that we'd never bothered to fix up. The pretty wallpaper had been stripped off because it was too sophisticated for children. I didn't see why Muffin and Baby Boy weren't just put in the third-floor room without going through all the furniture moving and wallpaper stripping, but Kate said it was too far away. (Twelve steps away, for heaven's sake.)

Dad and Kate asked me if I wanted to help fix up the new bedroom. (There were three new bedrooms to fix up, in fact. The kids' room, the new guest bedroom, and another little room at the end of the second floor hall which eventually would be Baby Boy's.) I said I'd be glad to work on the new guest room. They said we were doing Muffin's and Baby Boy's first. I said I'd rather not help. They said I should help anyway. I suggested wallpapering it black, and they left me alone.

Until yesterday. Then Dad insisted I pitch in. I was supposed to take down the old curtains and put them and the window seat cushions upstairs, get that darn rocker back out of the attic for Muffin, and line the bureau drawers. So far I had put the cushions upstairs.

The front stoop was becoming highly uncomfortable. I shifted position, being careful not to disturb Simon.

Dad and Kate had been on their honeymoon until two days ago, while Mrs. Meade had stayed at our house and taken care of me. The Wedding Queen had stayed with Muffin and Baby Boy in Kate's apartment. So I hadn't seen much of Kate or the kids recently, which was fine with me. But now they were moving in. What on earth would that be like?

The U-Haul turned onto our street and pulled up at the curb in front of our house. Well, I thought, they're here.

Everyone was climbing out of the station wagon. I sat where I was and watched as Muffin, dressed in a pink sunsuit and new white sneakers, her hair in ponytails (how cute could you get?), jumped out the back door and turned around to reach in for Rose-up, her rag doll.

Kate struggled out of the front seat with Baby Boy in his Snugli and the ever-present diaper bag, which held a lot more than diapers and seemed to be necessary whenever they were going further than the front yard.

"Hi, Kammy!" Muffin called cheerfully. "We're here!" She waved and I waved back. Then she waved Rose-up's hand and continued waving it until I yawned and said, "Hi, Rose-up," in my most bored voice.

"Hi, sweetie!" sang out my father. Everybody certainly was cheerful. "Come on and lend a hand."

"Hi, Dad," I said. I knew I had to help now. I placed Simon gently on the steps, hoping he'd stay asleep. But he didn't. He woke right up, took one look at all the people and boxes and bags, and made a scrambling dash for the shrubbery.

I took my time getting to the car. "Hi, Kate," I said, in a supreme effort at politeness. "Want me to take the baby?" As nuisancey as Baby Boy could be, I sort of liked him. When he wasn't crying, he was sweet and cuddly. I liked to hold him.

"Oh, no, that's O.K.," Kate answered quickly. "I'll take him. Why don't you grab some of the things in the back of the car? The bags are pretty light."

"I'm strong," I muttered.

"What?"

"I said O.K."

Two hours later, Dad, Mrs. Meade, Kate, Muffin, and I sat huffing and puffing on the back porch. The car and the U-Haul had been emptied, and each box, bag, and piece of furniture had been deposited in the appropriate room. Now everyone was sprawled in porch chairs (except for Baby Boy, who was reclining in his infant seat, holding his left foot with his hands, smiling, and drooling out of the corner of his mouth). Mrs. Meade had made lemonade, and we all sipped quietly, trying to cool off.

"Well," said Dad presently. He broke such a long silence that I jumped. Visibly. So I jumped again and scratched my back furiously, hoping I looked like I had a sudden, terrible itch.

"Why don't we," he continued, "forgo the unpacking and redecorating this afternoon and do something fun together?"

"That's a great idea!" exclaimed Kate. You'd have thought Dad had just come up with a substitute for oil. Kate must not know him too well, I smirked, or she'd know he does this every time he's faced with a large, unpleasant chore.

"What shall we do?" she asked.

"Go simming?" suggested Muffin. She surprised me. I guess I have a lot to learn about little kids. She'd been sitting quietly, sort of staring around. I had no idea she was following the conversation. Or maybe she wasn't. Maybe "simming" didn't mean what I thought it meant.

"Swimming, baby?" repeated Kate. "Well, it's not a bad idea. Is there some place nearby where we can swim, Robert?"

Please, please, *please* say no, I pleaded silently. Not the Community Pool. Or please suggest the beach, even though it's farther away.

"Sure," Dad said amiably. "Kammy and I always get a summer family membership at the Community Pool. We can all go. We can go every day this summer, if we want to."

I let out my breath in a slow, defeated sigh. Anywhere but the Community Pool. The problem with the CP was that it lived up to its name, and the entire community belonged. I was bound to see friends there, and the last thing I wanted to do was explain my enlarged family to everybody.

"Sounds great to me." Kate smiled. "I can't think of anything more divine right now than submerging myself in a large body of cold water."

Dad grinned at her, then at me. "What do you say, Kams? We haven't been yet this year. We can make a real splash there with our new family. Get it? *Splash?*"

"Oh," I groaned. "I got it, but I didn't want it." Dad is *so* corny. I was going to say I thought I'd stay home and read, but I knew he really wanted me to go. He wanted the five of us to be a family. He had said that several thousand times. So I didn't make a fuss. Anyway, I hadn't exactly acted enthusiastic about getting the little chair out of the attic, or carting all the boxes around in the heat, and I knew Dad's patience was wearing thin. I said I thought the pool sounded like a pretty good idea.

Dad and I had our getting-ready-for-the-pool preparations down to a science. We could go from fully dressed to suited up and in the car in ten minutes flat. Dad used to time us.

So today, when Dad said "pool," I flew into a whirlwind of activity and collapsed in the car nine and a half minutes later, gloating at having knocked thirty seconds off the record.

After two minutes I was still the only one in the car.

After five minutes I was still the only one in the car.

I let another two or three go by before I slid out of the front seat and headed curiously back inside. I knew they had not left without me. We do not own another car.

Upstairs I about fainted. The second floor was a shambles. I mean, half-unpacked boxes and suitcases never do much for a house anyway, but this was beyond a little untidiness and disorganization. It was chaos.

Muffin was dragging around in a Snoopy bathing suit with the straps unbuttoned. She was whining. I cannot begin to tell you what whining does to my ears.

Kate had managed to put on the top of her bikini but was still wearing her jeans and Nikes. She was carrying a squalling Baby Boy in her left arm and searching through a carton with her right.

Dad was changed completely, but he was hovering over the diaper bag. He looked up when I entered the overflowing hall. "I was in my suit and on my way to the car in under eight minutes," he told me sadly, "when Kate stopped me and indicated the mess they were in."

Dad and I exchanged worried glances.

"Well," I said, "there must be a way to speed things up a little. Otherwise it'll be next week before we get to the pool. What's holding everybody up?"

"I'm not sure if I have this all straight," Dad replied, "but it seems that nobody can button Muffin's straps the way Kate can, and that Muffin has to have her straps done *before* she can get together everything else she needs."

"What does she need besides a towel and Rose-up?"

"A *second* towel—and apparently only her farm-scene towel will do—her noseplug, her Mr. Bubble, her Horace the Inflatable Horse, and three or four other things I've forgotten."

"Oh, wow," I said, rolling my eyes.

"And that's not all. We have to get the diaper bag together—that's what I'm supposed to be doing—and Kate can't find her bikini bottom *or* the baby's bathing suit, and Muffin just squirted suntan lotion all over the bathroom floor and she's supposed to be cleaning it up, but I don't think she is," he wound up. He was out of breath.

"Couldn't we leave Baby B—, I mean the baby, here?" I suggested.

"No, I don't want to do that to poor Mrs. Meade just yet."

I could see what he meant.

So I heaved a huge sigh and pitched in. We were on our way in just under an hour and a half, far past the shank of the afternoon, as Dad would say, but I was not terribly concerned. Only bored. At least it was late enough so the pool crowd would be thinning out and I was less apt to run into someone I knew.

Dad also seemed pretty composed, considering he'd had to give up setting his new record and everything. He drove to the pool with a smile on his face, reminiscing about how harried life had been when *I* was little (although I personally did not recall ever being such a pain as Muffin) and declaring it would be just a matter of time before he could do Muffin's straps as well as Kate.

At the pool I scrambled through the gate and made a dash for our favorite spot, which is next to the diving pool, at a convenient distance from the snack bar and the water fountain. However, before I got halfway there, I heard Kate calling me.

I turned around.

"Kammy? Where are you going? Don't you want to sit with us?"

I walked back to them and looked from her to Dad.

"We *usually* sit by the diving pool," I said pointedly.

"Oh, but honey, it's much more convenient here. We're near the baby pool and the bathroom. We have to be near the bathroom. Muffin swallows a lot of water."

Dad shrugged his shoulders.

I was outnumbered.

So we spread all our stuff under a huge tree. (We weren't even in the sun, for pete's sake. How was I supposed to get a tan?) And we were next to the baby pool, where the average age of the swimmers was two and a half.

I wished harder than ever that no one would see me.

Kate took the kids (and Mr. Bubble and Mr. Inflatable Horsie and Mr. Diaper Bag) over to the little pool, and I lay on the grass with my entire body, including my head, covered by two large towels. Dad sat next to me in a lawn chair, reading a book that must have weighed thirty-five pounds.

"Kammy?"

"Yeah," I mumbled from between the grass and the terry cloth.

"You don't have to hide, you know. And you don't have to stick with us. You can go on over to the diving pool for a while."

"Are you sure Kate won't mind?"

"Yes. And if she does, she'll just have to accept the fact that you're almost a young adult, not a baby like Muffin, and you're entitled to certain privileges."

I uncovered my face and peered over at Dad.

"What privileges?"

"Well," he said, "you're entitled to your privacy. And you're entitled to any activities, friends, plans, and pets that were part of your life before Kate and I got married."

"I am?"

"Of course, pumpkin." Dad heaved his tome onto the lawn and turned to face me.

"Sweetie, Kate married me, and she and Muffin and Baby Boy have become part of our family, and yes, we're all going to have to make some concessions and do some adjusting. Even Baby Boy, and *Simon*, have to adjust in their own ways. But it does not mean our old way of life has ended. It's just sort of expanded. Kind of like"—he paused—"kind of like the difference between potato salad for two and potato salad for eighty-two. It takes more work to make it, and you might have to change the recipe a little, but it comes out tasting the same."

I eyed Dad carefully, trying to tell if he was kidding. Then I caught that funny wrinkle in his forehead that meant he was hiding a smile.

"Oh, Dad!" I laughed. "That was a *terrible* analogy."

"I know. I hope you understand what I'm saying, though."

"I think I do. Thanks." I leaned over and pecked him on the cheek. "I guess I will go to the diving pool. I see Jana and Rick there."

"O.K., Kams." He struggled to get the book back on his lap.

"You know what else I've learned from you?" I said.

"What?" he puffed.

"Never read anything you can't lift!"

Dad let out a guffaw, and I dashed off with my towel.

Jana and Rick were pals of mine from a couple of years ago when we all landed in the same advanced diving class at the Y. They live clear across town, in the other school district, so I never see them except during the summers, when we practically live in the diving pool. It had been exactly nine and a half months since we'd been together —the day the CP closed last year.

"Jana!" I called, running up the concrete path and waving like mad. "Rick! I'm here!"

"Kammy!" they shouted. Rick rose from his towel, where he'd been turning himself a nice shade of brown, and Jana hoisted herself out of the water, pulling off her bathing cap at the same time and shaking out her mane of black hair.

"Hey," we all cried, laughing and slapping each other on the backs.

"Look what I learned!" yelled Jana. In a second her cap was back on and she was flipping herself off the low board. Rick ran after her to try the dive, too, and I was right behind him.

We twisted and somersaulted and turned and jack-knifed and laughed and dripped. Finally we lay down in the sun, exhausted and steamy.

The last thing I was prepared for was a little voice near my left ear whispering, "Kammy, Kammy, Mommy wants you."

I sprung off my towel so fast I nearly toppled Muffin over. "I—I have to go," I said hastily.

"*Now*, Kam? Why? Who's that?" asked Rick, shading his eyes and squinting up at us.

"Nobody," I gulped. "Just—just a little kid from our street. I'll see you guys later."

I grabbed Muffin's wrist and trotted her off at a pace that was definitely too fast for her. I didn't stop until we were almost at our tree again.

Kate managed to tear herself away from some biology article she was reading long enough to say, "Oh, there you are, Kammy. I was wondering if you'd take over pool duty with Muffin for a few minutes. I'd like to go swimming for a bit while your dad stays in the shade with the baby."

I glared fiercely at Dad, but he was concentrating on diapering Baby Boy and didn't see me.

Before I could answer, Muffin, looking around uncertainly at all the adults, said, "Mommy? I don't want to go with Kammy. I want to go with you."

Honestly, it's amazing how she always figures out what the adults are discussing. Maybe she's just lucky. Whatever it was, she was solving my problem of having to be seen in the baby pool.

"Yes," I said, "why don't you and Dad take Muffin in the big pool, and I'll stay here with the baby?" I was

being crafty. I had a pretty good idea Kate would allow
no such thing.

She laughed nervously. "Oh, no, that's all right.
You're off pool duty, I guess."

I felt like picking a fight. "Come on, Kate," I pressed,
"you let me take care of Muffin but not B—, the baby."

"Kammy, you're *off pool duty,* O.K.?" she repeated.

"You already said that."

"Kamilla." That was Dad. It was his low, you're-
overstepping-your-bounds voice. He was such a stickler
for manners. And he hated unpleasantness. He'd rather
get an ulcer than fight with anyone. Mr. Mild-Man-
nered.

"But she doesn't trust me," I whined to Dad, realizing
somewhere in the back of my mind that I sounded like
Muffin.

"It's not that I don't trust you," Kate butted in, even
though an idiot, probably even Muffin, would have
known I was addressing my father, not her. "It's just that
he is still so tiny—an infant. Infants are not toys or dolls.
They need special care."

"And you don't trust me," I said again.

"Well . . . maybe I don't. You're only twelve. You
haven't done any serious baby-sitting . . ." She trailed off
and looked questioningly at my father.

Dad considered things for a few seconds and then
broke into this huge, false grin. "Let's *all* go to the big
pool," he suggested, standing up with Baby Boy in the
crook of his arm. Kate rose, too, but more slowly, and
took Muffin's hand.

"I'm staying here," I said loudly, and watched them
walk off together, all hand in hand.

I was so mad I sat and just fumed for a few minutes. Then I took a cheap plastic rattle out of the diaper bag, set it on Dad's book, put my shoe on top of it, and very slowly crushed it into fragments. I looked at them, brushed them all into the grass, and stalked off to the refreshment stand.

Even though it was four-thirty and even though I knew how Kate felt about red meat, I bought a foot-long hot dog and ate it under the tree. Kate caught me with the end of it and scolded me. But it didn't do her much good because I didn't answer her, and it's hard to yell very long at a person who doesn't fight back (another thing I learned from my father).

A good adjective to describe the entire pool outing is *rotten*. It was topped off during the ride home when Muffin threw up all over the back seat because she'd swallowed so much chlorinated water. I was never so glad to retreat to the safety of my bedroom.

CHAPTER 3

"I Can't Stand It!"

The next day was Sunday, Mrs. Meade's day off. I woke up at eight-thirty and staggered into the kitchen to fix breakfast. I have done this for Dad and me as long as I can remember, and I know just where everything is, and exactly what to do when, and how Dad likes everything.

This morning would not be quite the same, of course, with my "new" family, but I tried to keep Dad's words in mind—about how our life was more expanded than different. I set the kitchen table for four, put coffee mugs at two places and a milk glass at Muffin's, and set up Baby Boy's infant seat next to Kate.

By the time Kate came in, breakfast was ready. The coffee was perking, the orange juice was poured, and the whole wheat bread was waiting to be popped in the toaster.

I smiled at Kate, feeling a little guilty about having started the argument yesterday. "Good morning!" I said.

"Good morning, Kammy." Kate planted a kiss on the top of my head. "You're a sweetheart," she declared.

I grinned proudly, surveying my breakfast work.

"Thank you for starting breakfast. I'll finish up now. You run along."

"*Starting* breakfast? But Kate," I protested, "I've done everything. It's all finished. We just have to wait for Dad and Muffin."

"Don't you want eggs? Or cereal? Or fruit? I bought two beautiful cantaloupes yesterday. You need a healthy breakfast to start off the day."

I left in a huff and went sputtering off to find Dad. It wasn't hard. I followed a trail of Kleenexes and socks out to the back porch, where he was sort of collapsed on the chaise lounge, surrounded by the Sunday paper. He was still too bleary-eyed to read it. I couldn't tell whether he was fit to hold a conversation yet.

"Dad?" I asked uncertainly. I waited for his eyes to focus.

"Oh, good morning, Kams. How'd you sleep?"

"Just fine." I decided he was awake enough for a talk. "Um, Dad? You know how I always get breakfast on Sunday?"

"Yes?"

"Well, Kate's in the kitchen now, making this big production out of it, and she's fixing all these eggs and this melon and everything. Don't you like my breakfasts?"

"Oh, Kams," said Dad, wide awake now, "your breakfasts are *fine*. Kate's just adding to them. I'm going to have *your* toast and coffee and *her* eggs and melon—if I can fit it all in! I hope you're not going to stop doing your part, either. Kate makes dreadful coffee!"

"Really?" I asked.

"Really," he said firmly, and added, "putrid."

I giggled.

I didn't mind going in to breakfast then. And nobody said anything when all I ate was toast and juice. I *was* quite grossed out when Muffin laughed at something my father said and sprayed corn flakes all over the table, but in time, I hoped, I would learn to ignore things like that.

If I could have seen what the rest of the day was going

to be like, I might have been less cheerful. Looking back on breakfast, I understand now what is meant by the term "a false sense of security." Also the phrase "the calm before the storm."

Later that morning I rounded the corner from the front hall into the living room and fell over Muffin, who was sitting cross-legged on the floor with poor Simon in a headlock. Her free hand was patting him so hard his tummy was bouncing up and down. She was singing "Rock-a-Bye Baby."

"What are you doing?" I demanded.

Muffin released Simon guiltily, and he practically flew out of the room.

She opened her mouth to say something, but I cut her off. "Do you want to *kill* him?" I screeched. "He's only a kitten. You can't squeeze him and hit him." I had grabbed her arm and was shaking it with every word.

"I wuh-wasn't," Muffin wailed. A full-blown howl. "I was singiiiiiing." She drew out the last word long enough to attract Kate's and Dad's attention.

They ran in to find us face to face on the floor, Muffin bawling and me shaking her.

"All right, what's going on?" Kate was standing in the entryway, hands on hips. She looked from Muffin to me, then stooped to Muffin's level and brushed her tears away.

"You should have *seen* what she was doing to Simon," I whispered. "She was squeezing him and—and hitting him . . ."

"Oh," my father started to say, "well—"

"Muffin, sweetheart," Kate interrupted, "you have to be careful with the kitty. It's just a baby. You have to pat him very, very softly.

"And you, young lady," she went on, turning to me, "had better develop some patience. Muffin is about as much of a baby as Simon is—"

"Oh?" I said. "I thought her brother was the infant. He's the one I'm not old enough to be trusted with, remember?"

"Apparently," Kate said coldly, "you're not to be trusted with Muffin, either."

"Will everybody please quiet down?" Dad said suddenly, raising his voice for once. He looked like he surprised himself.

He lowered it quickly.

"Muffin, please be more careful with the cat. Kammy, please be more patient with Muffin. Is that clear? Yes? Then I don't want to hear another word about it." He turned and strode out of the room.

Kate and I exchanged astonished looks. "This is all *your* fault, you know," I said at last.

Before she could answer, I fled to find Simon.

That afternoon Dad gathered everyone for unpacking. That is how he accomplishes most things. He puts off a job until he feels guilty about it; then he rushes in, tackles it, and sticks with it until it's done. I wouldn't have been at all surprised if we'd worked until midnight.

Everyone was given a job. Dad and Kate unpacked and sorted the contents of the boxes. I put away Kate's kitchen stuff. Even Muffin put away her toys.

We had been working for a solid fifteen minutes when Baby Boy woke up from his fourth or fifth nap of the day and began crying.

"Ignore it," Kate said. "He'll drop back off."

But he didn't. The crying became yowling and the

yowling became shrieking. It was pretty hard to ignore.

"The neighbors are going to have us arrested for child abuse," I yelled from the kitchen.

Kate rose from her spot on the dining room floor and headed upstairs. Presently she returned carrying the squalling baby. "I hate to say this, everyone," (I decided never to preface anything with that comment), "but I think his colic is starting again."

Dad and I looked at each other blankly.

But Muffin actually *groaned*.

"What does that mean?" asked Dad warily.

"It means we better find what's left of his old soybean formula and start him back on that."

"That sounds simple enough," Dad said.

"But first he has to get over this bout of colic. He'll probably cry for several hours."

I could see why Muffin had groaned.

So the afternoon was spent finding Baby Boy's old formula, buying more of it, and walking him around.

I walked him until I got a headache.

I realized right then that back in the spring I should have come up with a Plan B for the summer, just in case living with my new family didn't work out. A Plan B is an alternative, which is always a safe thing to have.

I hadn't been able to come up with a Plan B, though. Dad and Kate had brought up the idea of camp several times, but I was pretty sure camp wasn't for me. I'm not the camping type. Give me a nice soft bed and a library full of books and I'm a satisfied person. But sleeping bags and mess halls—no, thanks.

I hadn't made too big a deal out of it, though. I had not, in fact, actually *said* I didn't want to go. This was because

I couldn't dream up any Plan Bs of my own. Camp was not my idea of a hot Plan B. It was not even a warm Plan B. It was just a plain Plan B. I would have to be pretty desperate to use it. But you never knew.

At the moment it did not sound too bad.

Baby Boy cried for four and a half hours. When he finished, the rest of us were more exhausted than he was. Muffin volunteered to take a nap at six o'clock, and slept until morning. Kate sat like a zombie in front of the TV set, which was unheard of. And Dad and I retired to the back porch.

We sat in silence for a while, listening to the crickets tune up and watching our yard turn gray with dusk. Simon got in Dad's lap. He looked sort of tired himself.

"Whew," I breathed finally.

"You can say that again."

"Whew," I repeated, and Dad grinned.

"That was quite an afternoon," he said.

"Yeah. Did I have colic when I was a baby?" I asked.

"You most certainly did not, and thank heavens for it."

I smiled.

Dad cleared his throat. There are only two occasions on which he does this—when he has a cold, and when he wants to discuss something. He did not have a cold now.

"Kams," he said rather stiffly, "I know this past year has not been easy for you—getting a stepmother, changing the special relationship you and I have, learning to live with a baby brother and sister—"

"*Step*brother and *step*sister," I corrected him.

"Whatever. The point is they've moved in. You're living with them. And suddenly you have to cope with things like colic and diapers and lost toys . . . Muffin not knowing how to treat Simon. . . . I told you yesterday that our old life isn't over. And it isn't, but there's no doubt it has changed. Tell me honestly, honey," he said suddenly, "how do you feel about all this?"

From the way he sort of blurted out the question, I could tell he had been deciding for a long time whether he should ask it. I thought awhile so I could give him my best, most honest answer.

"Well," I said slowly, "it's an awful lot to get used to. And mostly I wish it could be just you and me and Mrs. Meade like it used to be. Then sometimes Muffin does something funny, or the baby smiles at me, and I think that's kind of nice, too. . . . Do you remember that time I slept over at Jana's house, Dad? A couple of years ago?"

He nodded.

"Well, she has four brothers and a sister and two dogs. And everything at her house was so bustling and busy and happy with all the kids. It was a lot of fun. I sort of wished I had a big family. And now I have one, but it's not what I expected. If Kate could just get herself organized . . . oh, I don't know."

"I think I understand what you're saying," said Dad. "It will be better when we've settled into a routine. It's this getting-used-to-each-other business that's tough."

"Yeah," I agreed.

"You know, I was thinking again about camp for you. Even at this late date, we could get you into Camp Arrowhead. Remember Uncle Paul's sister-in-law's camp? If you wanted to go for the summer, you could avoid the settling down here. By the time you got back, things would be much calmer. Besides, camp would be a lot of fun. You could use some fun. What do you think?"

Plan B again. The only Plan B.

If I had to suffer through another weekend like this one with Baby Boy screaming and Muffin puking and Simon getting tortured and Kate yelling, I'd go crazy.

"I don't know," I said.

"Well, then, think it over. But not for too long. Camp will start in about two weeks."

"O.K.," I said. I really was going to think it over. It was a big decision.

I slept much later than usual the next morning and woke to see a bright June sun streaming in through the cracks between my window shades. I hopped out of bed and ran to the kitchen because I knew Mrs. Meade would be there. Dad, too, maybe, unless he had slept as late as I had. Summer session at the university didn't get under way until the beginning of July. He and Kate had a break until then.

Dad and Kate and Mrs. Meade were all there. "Morning, everybody," I cried, and gave Mrs. Meade a hug around her waist, which is big and very good for hugging.

I plopped into my chair, smiling. I could see Muffin playing in our backyard. Baby Boy was not around, but I didn't care where he was as long as he was quiet.

"Morning, chipper," said Kate. "It's a beautiful day, isn't it?"

"The best!" I said. "And you know what else kind of a day it is?"

"What kind?" asked Kate.

"I bet I know," said Dad. His eyes were twinkling.

"What?" I challenged him.

"A Marquand Park Day."

"Right! Can we go, Dad? Please?"

"I don't see why not. Maybe you and I could go by ourselves like we used to." He stared hard across the table at Kate. Whatever this was, they had discussed it before. I mean, I am not a dim person. And Dad was not being subtle.

"Why, that's a lovely idea," cried Kate, a little too enthusiastically.

"You can take a picnic," put in Mrs. Meade. "I'll pack you a lunch. Salad, pickles, brownies, lemonade. You can grill corn on the cob there."

I got so caught up in their excitement that I ran to my room to change, and before I knew it, Dad and I were on our bicycles, pedaling to the park. The breeze was in our faces and the sun filtered down through the trees, dappling our bodies with moving spots. With Muffin and Baby Boy out of the way, I felt so happy and free I thought I'd burst.

At the park Dad and I staked out our old table. We usually take a picnic to Marquand two or three times a summer. It's a big, grassy, shady park with a playground and tables and fireplaces and a dark wood to walk through. I named it Witches' Wood when I was six and still believed in such things.

Dad had his fancy camera along and kept yelling, "Say cheese, sweetie!" He caught me upside-down on the monkey bars, dripping wet after a round with the trick water fountain, perched on Old Brown's Pine Tree, which happens to have a branch shaped like a seat, sitting on a swing with my hair flying behind me, and holding up a thoroughly charred ear of corn.

"Oh," he groaned later as we polished off Mrs. Meade's huge lunch. "I feel like stuffed pork."

"Me, too. I can't move."

"Let's digest and then take a walk through Witches' Wood."

"O.K.," I said, and reached for the book I'd brought along.

Dad stood up. "I'm just going to make a quick phone call," he said. "I want to call Kate and make sure the baby's O.K."

Swell, I thought. It's impossible to escape them. But I was reading *The Lion, the Witch, and the Wardrobe* and soon forgot—until I looked up and saw Dad pounding across the grass toward me. He almost never runs.

Oh, no, I thought. What now?

"Pumpkin," said Dad, looking both frantic and apologetic. "I'm afraid we've got to go back. The baby's colic seems to be worse instead of better, Muffin is missing and Mrs. Meade's out looking for her, and any minute the slipcover man is going to show up to measure the couches."

I slammed my book shut. Then I crammed all our stuff in the picnic basket.

"Kammy, these things can't be helped."

" 'Course not."

It is hard to speak when you are gritting your teeth. We got our bikes and rode home.

By the time we got there, things were already better. Baby Boy was crying—I could hear him from the garage —but it wasn't as bad as yesterday, when he could have waked the dead. The slipcover man had arrived and was measuring the couches all by himself. And Mrs. Meade was in the kitchen having a cup of tea, which must have meant Muffin was found. I sat down to talk to her while Dad went off to relieve Kate.

"Where was she?" I asked.

"Muffin? Oh, just down the street. She found a little boy about her age, and they were playing in his sandbox. She gave me a good scare, though. She's up taking a nap now, poor thing. All worn out."

If *I* had ever run off, Mrs. Meade would have tanned my hide, not called me "poor thing."

I left the kitchen and stomped upstairs. I stomped right into the bathroom, where I planned to drown my sorrows in a bubble bath.

But I stopped in horror.

Muffin, "poor thing," was not taking a nap. She was not even lying on her bed. What she was doing was kneeling in front of the toilet, pouring my poster paint powder in the bowl, and flushing repeatedly, watching the colors swirl away.

This time I did not shake her or yell at her. I merely tiptoed out of the bathroom and let out a shout that could have deafened Goliath.

"*Dad! Kate!*"

Not until Baby Boy started crying did I realize that somebody had probably just managed to get him to sleep.

Anyway, I scared Muffin and she started bawling, too. Then Dad and Kate and Mrs. Meade all ran into the hall. Mrs. Meade looked frightened, Dad looked worried, and Kate looked angry. Her face was a thundercloud.

But I didn't stop screaming. "Look at this! Look at her!" I yelled. "I can't stand it. I *can't stand* it."

Kate grabbed my wrist and jerked it. "What's *wrong* with you?" She wasn't yelling, but I'd never heard anybody sound quite so angry. "Do you always feel you've got to create a scene? Do you ever think of anyone beside yourself? I should have thought *you*, of all people, would have noticed the peace and quiet; the baby finally fell asleep."

"That's just it," I answered right back. "I didn't notice anything because I'm not used to having a baby around. Just like I'm not used to having my paints flushed down the toilet or my cat tortured, or being barfed on in the car, or sitting by the baby pool with two-year-olds. Talk about thinking of other people, did you two think about me or Muffin when you decided to get married? Did you ask *us* if we wanted this? No. Well, I'll tell you something. I'm not putting up with it. I can't stand it. And somebody better do something about it."

With as much dignity as I could possibly muster, I turned, walked to my room, closed the door, and locked it.

The house was quiet except for Baby Boy.

CHAPTER 4

Plan B

About ten minutes after I had exploded in the hall, I heard a soft knock at my door. It was so soft I couldn't even tell if it was a real knock, and thought it might be Simon scratching. I slid off my bed and opened the door.

Muffin stood there, tear-stained and miserable. "I'm sorry about your paints," she said. She turned and started to run off down the hall, but I grabbed her by the collar of her shirt and pulled her into my room.

She looked terrified. I didn't blame her, considering.

"It's O.K., Muffin." I felt sorry for her, looking so scared, and I was pretty sure apologizing was her own idea, since she'd come alone. Besides, ever since Baby Boy was born, and especially since his colic had kicked up, Kate spent about as much time with Muffin as Dad did with me. I hadn't thought about it until now. Maybe she was lonely. Not that I wanted to get stuck with her or anything.

"Listen," I said, "I'll make a deal with you. You know what a deal is?"

Muffin nodded solemnly.

She really was smart. Thank goodness, because I don't know how I would have explained the meaning of "deal" to her.

"O.K., here's the deal. You promise not to touch my

things without asking me first, and I promise not to yell at you anymore. Is that a deal?"

Muffin thought this over for several seconds. "Any of your things?" she asked.

"Without asking first," I repeated. "I might let you use them. Just ask, that's all."

"O.K.," she said, nodding her head.

"Thanks, Muffin." I grinned at her, and she smiled back tentatively. Then she disappeared down the hall.

I closed my door again, but did not bother to lock it.

About ten minutes after that, another knock came at the door. It was louder and higher up. Not Muffin.

"Come in," I called anyway.

Dad and Kate entered together, looking grim. The last time my father looked this grim was when our phone service was cut off because I made so many goof calls, the operator caught up with me.

Considering their grimness, I pulled an old trick and apologized before either one could say anything.

"I'm sorry," I said. "I'm sorry I was thoughtless and woke the baby and scared Muffin."

Dad looked like I had lifted a ten-ton weight from his back. He even smiled. Then he sat down on my bed, with Kate hovering anxiously behind him.

"I'm sorry, too," she said. "I guess we both said things we didn't really mean."

I thought back over what I had said and decided she was wrong. I meant every word.

"And I guess I haven't been very patient with you, Kammy," she continued. "Look at me." She gave a disgusted little laugh. "Yesterday I scolded you for not being patient with Muffin, and all along I wasn't practicing what I was preaching. I really am sorry."

"That's O.K.," I said.

"Things certainly don't seem to be getting off to a very smooth start." Kate sat down on the bed looking dangerously close to tears. Dad reached for her hand and held it tight, but spoke to me.

"Well, I think some of our problems are solved, anyway," he said. "I just called the camp. They can make room for you. And it starts even sooner than we thought. We'll drive up this Sunday. You can stay for eight weeks, almost the whole summer. It's the only way I can think of to get you out of this situation. And I do think everything will be better, much better, by the time you get back. We'll have unpacked, settled into a routine . . ."

I didn't know quite what to say. I couldn't say I wanted to stay home now, not after my scene in the hall.

On the other hand, I had pretty much decided camp was not for me.

I took the plunge.

"Dad," I said, carefully keeping the shakiness out of my voice. "I've been thinking about camp, and I've decided I don't really want to go."

"What? But we've been talking about it all spring. You never said you didn't want to go. And now, today, you seemed so unhappy. . . . I thought you wanted to get away."

"I do," I said, with a lot less conviction than when I had yelled at Kate, "but I don't want to go to a place where I don't know anybody. I don't want to sleep in a strange bed and have to do things I'm no good at like volleyball and baseball and tennis."

"Let me get this straight," said Dad. "You're not happy here now."

"Right," I said. That was the honest truth. Even if Muffin wasn't going to touch my things anymore, I still had to put up with her whining and barfing, and the trips to the baby pool, and the colic, and always being late, and Kate—especially Kate. She came on hot and cold like a faucet. I didn't know *what* to make of her.

"So," he continued, "wouldn't you like to get away for a while, until things settle down?"

"Maybe."

"But you don't want to go to camp."

"Right."

"Do you have any other suggestions?"

I thought a minute. "Visit Aunt Noël and Uncle Sheldon in Trumbull?"

"They're in Europe this summer. Noël's on sabbatical."

"I could join them in Europe."

"Nice try." Dad laughed.

"Stay with Granny and Grandpoppy?"

"Honey, two years ago we'd all have jumped at the idea. But now I think it would be too much for them. They're simply not well enough."

This is true. My mother's parents, the only grandparents I have left, are getting sort of frail and forgetful. They have these two stodgy, live-in housekeepers. A summer with them would not be all that much fun anyway.

I was rapidly running out of ideas. This was pretty much the way my Plan B brainstorming sessions had gone.

"Kammy, the camp sounds wonderful," said Kate. "It's in Connecticut in a very pretty, woodsy part of the state. You can swim, ride horses, take hikes, learn to canoe. It's a super place. It has everything."

I kept my mouth shut.

"Would you be willing to try something?" she went on.

"I don't know. Maybe. What?" At this point I'd have tried summer school.

"Would you agree to try camp for two weeks? There's a parents' visiting day after two weeks. When we come up then to see you, you can come home if you really aren't happy. We'd work something out. Or you could try just living here again. But at least give camp a try."

What a choice. "Living here again" sounded more like a threat than an option.

I felt like sticking Kate with one of Baby Boy's diaper pins. The problem was that it was such a reasonable offer. If I said no, I'd look like the World's Biggest Baby.

I decided it all boiled down to Camp *versus* Home. The Great Unknown versus The Horrible Known. I thought about it for a minute. Maybe the unknown would turn out to be better than the known. Maybe. I decided it was worth a shot—but I wasn't going to enjoy trying it.

At dinner that night, Dad was in a rare mood. He looked very relieved. Was I that much of a problem?

When we were all seated and Mrs. Meade had filled our plates, he actually stood up and made a toast.

"Here's to us," he said, holding out his water glass.

Kate held hers out, and Muffin copied her.

I stared at my lap. It already had crumbs in it.

"Hear, hear," said Kate.

"Hear, hear," said Muffin.

Baby Boy burped in his infant seat.

I hoped we could get on with dinner.

"Well, it's all arranged," said my father as he sat down again. I don't think he noticed that I had chosen not to participate in the toast. "We'll drive up to Camp Arrowhead on Sunday."

I didn't say anything. I examined my peas.

"Oh," said Dad suddenly, "I should have shown you the pamphlets we have on it. Paul sent them a few weeks ago. I wonder where I put them. Anyway, they describe the activities and the area, and have photos of the cabins and the lake and things. I'll try to find them after dinner."

"Kammy, I really do think it will be fun," said Kate. "A whole summer with lots of different things to do. Have you ever been boating or water skiing? You can go swimming in the lake every day, play tennis. Don't those things sound like fun?"

"They're not high on my list of priorities." I had never picked up a tennis racket in my life.

Dad coughed. It was not a true cough. I was treading on thin ice.

Kate wouldn't give up. "There's a terrific arts and crafts program. You'd like that. Pottery, weaving, woodworking, needlework, metal shop."

I bit my lip. I did like arts and crafts. A whole lot.

"And horseback riding," she added. "I know you like horses."

She had me there. I *love* horses. More than anything. And every person at that table knew it.

"Yes, I like horses."

"Good, good," said my father. "Now, you and Kate and Mrs. Meade and I have less than a week to get you ready. We'll bring the footlocker down from the attic.

And you'll need some new things. I think a tennis outfit, and certainly a sleeping bag, right, Kate?"

Kate nodded and smiled.

"And like I said, we'll drive up on Sunday." He seemed awfully delighted about sending me to Camp Arrowhead.

Well, *he* may have been happy about dumping me up there, and *Kate* may have been happy about dumping me up there, but I was not going to be happy about dumping me up there. I had said I would go. That was all. I didn't have to be happy about it.

Why were *they* so happy, anyway? Was it really because they thought I'd be happy? Or was it because they didn't want me around?

They had a perfect family without me—mother, father, daughter, son. Four beautiful, happy people. Where did I fit in? Was I ruining their little family? I certainly hadn't improved it any. Maybe they didn't want me around. Maybe this was just Step 1. Step 2 would be boarding school. After that—who knew? I didn't even want to think about it. Camp was scary enough. *Two weeks, maybe even eight!* The longest I remembered being separated from my father was when I was seven and he went to a convention, and I spent two nights at my grandparents' house. (They lived next door at the time.)

I was scared of living with strangers and of swimming in a lake. (Snakes swim in lakes, too, and with their whole bodies under water so there is no way you can see them in time.) I was scared of trying new sports and new foods. (Who, besides Mrs. Meade, knew that the only way I can eat a fried egg is if the yolk is broken so it gets cooked, too?) What if I got sick? What if the other campers teased me? What if I made a fool of myself? This was going to be some summer. A bummer summer.

I finished my dinner in silence.

The next day was Tuesday. That was the day the Great Camp Preparations began. Kate took me to the Quakerbridge Mall for a shopping spree. (That was her term for it. Mine was bribery.) It was supposed to be fun. Muffin and Baby Boy stayed home (to Muffin's surprise and dismay) so Kate and I could go alone together and have lunch and everything.

I was not in a fun frame of mind. Which meant that I was not going to find things I liked. Shopping is a chore, and you have to be mentally prepared for it. Kate was prepared. She felt like fun.

We went to this clothing store first. Kate was under the impression that I needed three sports shirts, preferably with alligators on the fronts. I didn't see what was wrong with my "South of the Border" T-shirt, but at this point, clothes were the least of my problem.

After I looked through three racks of shirts in my size and rejected every one of them, Kate began to appear a tiny bit miffed.

"Kammy, there must be something here you like."

"Not really," I said.

She frowned at me. She's a very good frowner. Lots of wrinkles. "Please don't be difficult. You need new clothes. You've grown a lot this year. Look. Look at this shirt." She pulled a pink-and-white striped one with an alligator off the rack. "Isn't this cute?"

Cute. I am not a cute person. I wrinkled my nose. "I don't know. Not really."

"All right," said Kate. "If you're not going to help, I'll have to choose for you."

"O.K.," I said. "I'm going to play Pac-Man." The store was equipped with a Pac-Man game for shoppers' bored children.

Kate gave me a look that could have killed a snake. "I really am," she said.

"O.K. Will you be long?" I was asking for it.

Kate did not dignify the question with an answer. I had to give her credit for that. She whipped around and marched off in the direction of the alligators.

I did not see her again until I had spent $1.50 on games. When she came back she was all smiles.

"Hi, there," she said.

I dragged myself away from the little biting fish. I know it's not a fish, but that's what Pac-Man looks like.

"Look what I found for you." She held the bag open as we left the clothing store and got on an escalator.

I peeked inside. I saw a lot of pink and lime green and one or two alligators. "That's nice," I managed. "I'll try them on at home."

Kate sighed.

I will not go into the rest of the details of the "shopping spree." Mostly they are boring. Pretty much the same thing happened at the shoe store, the sports store, and the Quakerbridge Luncheonette. I gave in to Kate right down the line, but not until after I'd given her a hard time.

When it was all over I had the three alligator shirts, a tennis outfit, a pair of Nikes, six pairs of white socks, a sleeping bag, a canteen, a mess kit, two Speedo bathing suits, and a bathing cap. (Plus a salad for lunch.) What

I had wanted was an "I'm a heartbreaker" T-shirt and roller skates. (Plus cheesecake for lunch.) But what I wanted didn't seem to count.

Kate did not speak to me on the way home.

On Wednesday, Mrs. Meade and Kate lugged the black footlocker out of the attic. It had these nice brass fastenings. (The footlocker, I mean; not the attic.) They began packing very carefully. The packing lasted three days.

On Saturday I decided to stay in bed. Dad stuck his head in the door around noon. "Come on, Miss Slug-a-Bed. Up and at 'em!"

He is incredibly corny at times.

"Dad," I mumbled from under my pillow, "I don't feel too well."

"Let me feel your forehead, honey."

I emerged from under my pillow.

"You're fine," he pronounced. What did he think he was—a faith healer?

I started to protest.

"Kammy," he said gently, sitting on the edge of the bed.

I rolled over on my back and looked at him.

"We have a compromise. Your part of the bargain is to try camp for two weeks, right?"

I kept my mouth shut and rolled back over on my stomach. I didn't say a word until we arrived at Camp Arrowhead the next day.

CHAPTER 5

Camp Arrowhead

Three hours is a very long time not to speak to somebody when you and that person are alone together in a car. That was why the ride to Camp Arrowhead seemed to take more like three days.

Everybody in our house, even Baby Boy, had gotten up at five-thirty that morning. Nobody complained. If I had been speaking I might have complained, but I was not speaking. To anybody.

Except Simon. He understood. He had spent Saturday night with me, his little body all curled up by my neck. When Simon is that near my ear, his purr is quite loud. Louder than you'd think a ten-week-old kitten could possibly purr. I talked to Simon and told him my feelings about camp. He smiled a cat smile, which meant he understood.

Kate cooked a huge breakfast for us—orange juice, bacon, eggs (any way you wanted—I didn't get any since I wouldn't say what I wanted), and danish or toast.

Muffin wanted to know why she'd been waked up. "Why are we up so early, Mommy?" she kept asking. Kate tried to explain about camp. (For a smart kid, Muffin was sure acting slow. Nobody had talked about anything except camp for a solid week). But all Kate succeeded in doing was scaring her. "Am I going, too?"

Muffin asked. She looked like she might cry. Again.

At that point I considered opening my mouth to say, "Why, yes, Muffin, of course you're going. You're going to another camp. Camp Blockhead. You're going to stay there for three or four months. Without your mother."

I was really torn, but in the end I decided it was more important to keep up the silent treatment.

At seven-thirty Dad and the footlocker and I got in our station wagon.

Kate stood on the front porch of our house burping Baby Boy. Muffin stood beside her in a yellow night-gown and her pink bunny slippers, solemnly holding Rose-up. They waved and called out, "Good-bye, Kammy! Good-bye! Have a great time."

I stared straight ahead of me. I did not move a muscle.

We started driving and Dad tried small talk for about six minutes. Then he resorted to the radio. He pushed the button for classical music. I pushed the button for WORM. Dad kept on driving. We listened to WORM all the way to Camp Arrowhead.

The first thing I saw at camp was people. A whole fleet of them. Their cars were parked in a big parking lot. All across it and in this grassy area next to it were mothers and fathers and children and babies and counselors. There were about eighty-five other station wagons and footlockers. I was glad Kate had painted my name on my footlocker.

"Oh, my Go—," I started to say. I was saying it under my breath, but as it was the first thing I'd said in about twenty-four hours, my father heard it.

"Kamilla," he warned.

"Well, I'm sorry," I said, "but look at all these people."

"It is sort of a mob scene," he agreed. I think he was glad I was talking again.

Before we had extricated ourselves from the car, a counselor greeted us. I assumed she was a counselor anyway. She was wearing a CAMP ARROWHEAD T-shirt and had a whistle around her neck. Also, she was carrying a clipboard.

"Hi," she said. She was perky. I wasn't sure how I felt about a perky person. Perky is almost as bad as cute.

"Hello," said my father, sticking out his hand. "This is Kamilla Whitlock, and I'm her father, Robert Whitlock."

"I'm Susan," said the girl. "Nice to meet both of you." She checked her clipboard. "Kamilla Whitlock. O.K., your counselor this summer will be Nancy. Nancy Hirsch. She's over there wearing the yellow shirt. Just leave your trunk by your car and we'll see that it gets to your cabin. Nancy will help you with everything else."

"Thank you," said Dad. He heaved the trunk out of the back and stood it on its end, out of everyone's way.

Then we started across the lot for Nancy. I had butterflies in my stomach. I thought I might even throw up. But I took a few deep breaths and calmed down.

"Hi," said Nancy as we stepped up to her. "You must be either Kamilla Whitlock or Emily Marshall. Everyone else has checked in already." She smiled. It was a nice smile.

"I'm Kamilla," I said, and hesitated, not knowing whether to tell her about my name. But she solved that problem for me.

"Kamilla. That's a pretty name," she said. "Is that

what you like to be called, or do you have a nickname?"

I like people who give you choices and listen to you. She didn't ask me what I'm called. She asked me what I *like* to be called. I could have said Tulip Bernice Vanessa and it would have been all right with her, as long as it was all right with me. "Everyone calls me Kammy."

Suddenly I remembered Dad. "And this is my father," I said awkwardly. I am not very good at introductions.

"Nice to meet you," said Nancy, smiling her nice smile again.

Nancy started explaining what we were supposed to do next. It wasn't too hard. Just go over to the lawn by the mess hall, where there seemed to be some sort of ongoing picnic lunch, eat, and wait for Nancy. Dad could leave whenever he felt like it.

I watched Nancy as she talked. Her best feature was her lack of cuteness. She was attractive, but not cute. No button nose, no dimples, and a few interestingly crooked teeth; short, dark hair that fell to her shoulders, and no barrettes or headbands or pink ribbons. So far so good.

Dad and I left her and walked off in the direction she had pointed out. We followed a gravel path through a little woodsy area. A few signs directed you to the mess hall, the cabins, the lake, and the stables. All the signs were the brown wood kind with the letters carved in and painted yellow. They stood on short stakes. Very rustic.

Dad and I followed a bunch of other campers and their families along the path. I wanted to talk to Dad, but I didn't quite know how, after all those hours of silence.

"Dad, look out!" I called as he approached a tree root. It was about an inch tall. Perfect tripping height. "You don't want to break another toe," I said. He hadn't broken a toe since Thanksgiving.

Dad stepped gingerly over the root, looked down at me, and flashed me a rueful grin. He reached for my hand. But I wasn't quite ready for that. I drew back.

We emerged into the sunshine. A big building stood before us. It was built out of the same brown wood as the signs. And it was carefully labeled MESS HALL (just so nobody would mistake it for the lake or the stables). Beyond the mess hall was a herd of people.

Dad and I walked over to where four long tables loaded with food were set up. I saw sandwiches and hamburgers and hot dogs and potato salad and watermelon and cupcakes and lemonade. I was not the least bit hungry.

Dad took a plate and filled it. Piled it, to be exact. Sometimes I am amazed at his appetite. I dragged along behind him with an empty plate.

"Come on, Kams," he coaxed. "Eat up. You may never see the likes of this again. It even beats our barbecues."

"I'll eat later," I said.

"You'll probably have to wait until dinner."

"That's O.K." I felt numb. "Dad, how are we ever going to find Nancy in all this?"

"Don't worry, pumpkin. She said she'd find you." Dad stood with his plate of food and looked around for a space big enough for the two of us to sit down. We finally found a tiny patch of grass and wedged ourselves between a fat family and a family with six children.

I watched everyone eat. It was sort of gross.

Suddenly a bell rang. It went off like an Oriental gong. They probably heard it in North Dakota.

It was quite effective. All the voices died down, and I saw a sea of faces turn toward the mess hall.

A woman was standing on a stool. "Welcome to Camp Arrowhead," she announced. I was expecting a booming voice to go along with the bionic gong, but she had a pleasant sort of shout.

"I am Mrs. Wright, the director. I'm very pleased to see all of you here today." She went on for a while about how this was the twenty-third year the camp had been in session and how many activities it had now and stuff. Then she said some things that were supposed to reassure the parents, like how all the counselors had taken Red Cross first aid and knew lifesaving, and how the nurse was a *trained RN* (I never heard of an untrained one), and how a local doctor was on call twenty-four hours a day.

Finally she announced that in about half an hour, when we'd had time to finish eating and *clean up* (hint, hint), each counselor would call out the names of her campers and we'd all go to our cabins and unpack.

Everyone clapped for Mrs. Wright. I looked around and saw a lot of parents leaving. Dad had finished eating.

"Well, I guess you might as well go now," I said.

Dad looked a little uncertain. "All right . . ."

We both stood up and looked at each other. Finally I stuck out my hand. "See you," I said.

"Oh, Kammy." Dad didn't take my hand. His voice was husky. "Kammy, I wish you'd give just a little. I can't figure you out. I thought you needed to be apart from the family. Now I don't know whether you'd be

more miserable here or at home. Look, I'll leave it up to
you. If you want to come home now, that's fine. Really."

"No, no," I said stiffly. "We have a *compromise*, right?
I have to hold up my end of the bargain." I crossed my
arms and looked him straight in the eye.

"O.K.," said Dad. He sounded tired. "We'll call you
soon. The pamphlet says parents can call between seven
and eight-thirty any night."

I shrugged my shoulders. "O.K."

"Good-bye, pumpkin," said Dad.

"Bye."

"Kate put stamps in your trunk. We'd love to get a
letter."

"O.K."

"We'll talk soon."

"O.K."

Finally he turned and joined the stream of parents
who were walking back to the parking lot. I watched
him stride away, head down, hands jammed in his
pockets.

I sat down. I didn't have the vaguest idea what to do
with myself. I checked my watch. Twenty more minutes
before the counselors were going to round us up.

I looked around. With the parents and families leaving, the crowd had thinned out considerably. I saw a lot
of other kids sitting alone. Even so, I felt uncomfortable.
Especially because there were several chatty groups of
kids who already knew each other. They laughed and
joked and did not pay attention to anyone but themselves. They had probably been born at Camp Arrowhead.

I kept my eye on the nearest group of girls until the gong sounded again.

One by one the counselors stood on Mrs. Wright's stool and called out six names.

Nancy was the eighth counselor up.

"Jan Aronson," she called out.

I watched a girl close to the mess hall stand up and trot over to Nancy.

"Susan Benson," Nancy shouted. "Emily Marshall. Angela Phillips. Mary Rhodes. Kammy Whitlock."

I am used to being last.

I joined Nancy and the other girls, and she shooed us off to a quiet spot. She ran through the names again. I knew I would forget them all by the time we reached the cabin. My memory is not always great, particularly with names.

Nancy led us along another gravel path. This one went up a small hill away from the front of the mess hall. As soon as our path started heading uphill, the woods began and the gravel ended. We passed a sign that said UPPER GIRLS.

Upper girls' what? I wondered. I would have asked Nancy, but she was talking to a thin, curly-headed girl. Every piece of the girl's clothing, including (no joke) her socks, had an alligator on it. I couldn't remember her name. Emily? Susie? Ruth? Did we have a Ruth? The girl talked to Nancy like they were old friends. She was probably one of those campers who had grown up here.

The rest of us didn't say much. At one point I heard a funny noise behind me. I turned around. The girl in back of me was sniffing and rubbing her eyes and trying to look like she wasn't crying.

"Hey," I said. I'm a sucker for tears. Unless they're Muffin's. "Hey, what's the ma—?"

I stopped. The girl behind the girl who was crying was waving her arms and pointing at her eyes and shaking her head.

What? What did that mean? The crying girl had an eye problem? The crying girl was crazy?

"What's your name?" I asked instead. "I'm really bad at names. I've already forgotten everyone's. Mine's Kammy." When I am nervous, I babble.

"Mary," said the girl. Her voice shook. "Mary Rhodes."

"I've never been to camp before," I said.

"Neither have I," whispered Mary.

"This is my fourth summer here," said the girl who had waved her arms. "A lot of new kids are here this year. Don't worry," she added. "You'll have fun. You'll make friends fast."

I could not remember her name either. I decided I would not embarrass myself by asking again.

Ahead of us Nancy had stopped. She was opening the door to a cabin off the right side of the path. A sign over the door said MISTY MOUNTAINS. Cute.

"Home sweet home," Nancy announced, grinning.

We all walked in. It was rustic and woodsy. It looked uncomfortable.

I have never been partial to bunks. But there they were. Three sets of them, built into the walls. Our trunks had been placed by them.

The room was L-shaped. The end part had a cot and a bureau and a chair and could be closed off with a curtain. Nancy's room probably.

The girl who had waved her arms turned out to be Emily. And she and I ended up as bunkies. This was because after a lot of whispering between Nancy and the curly-headed alligator girl (Susie), Susie asked Mary to be her bunkie. I think Nancy wanted Mary paired up with an old-timer. Then Jan and Angela immediately chose each other. They were friends from last year. So that left Emily and me.

The first thing we were supposed to do was get organized. I got organized in a hurry. I hate getting organized.

I sat on my bed and dangled my legs over the side. I had the top bunk. Emily said we should switch after four weeks.

Emily got organized pretty fast herself. She climbed up the ladder to my bed and sat down next to me.

"Here," she said. She pulled a pack of Juicy Fruit out of her shorts pocket and handed me a piece.

"Thanks."

"Have you ever been away from home before?" she asked.

I shook my head.

"Do you think you'll be homesick?"

I shrugged my shoulders. "I don't know. I didn't want to come here. My father and stepmother sent me here. To get me out of the way."

"Oh."

Emily's solemn brown eyes were studying me carefully.

"They just got married," I added. "And Kate has these two little kids and they moved into our house and I didn't fit in with them."

"I just have my parents and one big brother," said

Emily. "My brother is sixteen. His name is Mason. He eats like a horse."

I giggled.

"How come you let your parents make you come here?" she asked.

"It's sort of a long story," I said. "Actually, after we'd gotten here, Dad said I could come home. But I didn't want him to think I'm a chicken, so I said no."

Emily nodded thoughtfully.

I decided to leave out the part about how I might go home in two weeks.

"Hey," I said, lowering my voice. I checked around to make sure no one was listening to us. Nancy was behind the curtain, and the other four were still getting organized. (Susie was getting the most organized of all. There must be some camp tricks I do not know about. She had been rearranging her trunk for fifteen minutes.)

"What?" whispered Emily.

"What were you trying to tell me when I started to talk to Mary before?"

"I just didn't want you to say anything about crying. You should have seen her when her parents left. I was right next to them. Mary was crying so hard she couldn't stop. It took her forever to get calmed down. I didn't want her to start up again. I hope she's going to be all right this summer."

"She's here for the whole summer?"

"Mm-hm. I asked her."

"What about Susie?" I whispered after awhile. "Do you know her from before?"

"Yes, and she is one huge pest. This is about her sixth summer here. She thinks she knows everything. She is

Little Miss Perfect—in good with all the counselors and Mrs. Wright, never makes a mistake, and does things like regularly volunteering for trash detail. You will grow to hate her."

"Yuck," I said.

"Definitely," agreed Emily.

"And what about Jan and Angela?"

"They're O.K. They're best friends from last summer. I bet their parents had to sign them up in January to get them in the same cabin. Sometimes they act like there's no one at camp except themselves. Jan can be really nice, though. She's a good rider and she'll help you with the horses if you ever need it. And Angela is good at arts and crafts. If she paid as much attention to her projects as she does to her nails, she'd do terrific work."

I checked Angela's nails. They were fuchsia.

The curtain across Nancy's part of the room was suddenly flung over to one side.

"O.K., girls," said Nancy. "It's a free-for-all this afternoon. You can do whatever you want: swim, ride the horses, play softball, take the canoes out. It will give you a chance to find out where everything is—or to refresh your memory," she added hastily, glancing at Susie, who had been about to protest. "Just be at the mess hall at six o'clock."

I sighed. I did not want to leave the cabin. I do not like lakes or boats or softball. I wanted to read. And I did not want to be a leech on Emily.

"Come on," said Emily, scrambling down the ladder. "Time for the fun to begin."

I wanted to crawl into my sleeping bag and zipper myself in.

I cleared my throat. "I am really not too good at any of those things," I said. I could feel tears starting. I hoped I wouldn't embarrass myself by crying.

"It doesn't matter," smiled Emily. "I'll just show you around, then. You might be surprised."

"O.K." I took a Kleenex out of my pocket, quickly swiped at my eyes, and stuffed it away again. I climbed down the ladder, and Emily and I walked out of the cabin together.

CHAPTER 6

Trouble

On Monday morning I woke up with the birds. To be more exact, I woke up because of the birds. They started singing around four-thirty and were very hard to ignore. Of course, we have birds at home, but not as many. This is understandable since we do not live in a forest.

Hundreds, possibly thousands of birds had all settled down around Misty Mountains to roost for the night. I thought of a scary movie I saw on TV once called *The Birds*. In the movie these huge flocks of gulls and things turn nasty. Then they run amok and attack the people in a little sea town.

I shivered and sat up in bed. I checked out the window for psychotic birds. Then I checked my watch. It was only five o'clock. The last time I was awake at five was in January when I had the stomach flu and had to throw up.

I lay back down and tried to get comfortable. This was not easy. I may have mentioned that I am not partial to bunk beds. Or sleeping bags. Or windows without shades.

I thought about yesterday. It had not been quite so bad after all. At least until the night. Emily was really nice. And fun. She walked me all over camp and showed me everything and introduced me to a few girls she knew from other years.

The arts and crafts cabin was really neat. It had more
equipment than I had ever seen under one roof: two
kilns, four pottery wheels, and best of all, rows of cupboards overflowing with materials. I was in heaven. I
could have spent all afternoon just standing there smell-
ing the clay and paint and wood and glue. It was a damp,
friendly smell. Even if I hated everything else about
Camp Arrowhead, I knew I would love that cabin. De-
spite the fact it was named Sunny Skies.

I was not too thrilled with the tennis courts. Or the
lake or the boathouse. But I liked the stable. (It was called
Haven, which I thought was sort of strange. Why not
Horse Haven or something? Maybe part of the sign had
fallen off.)

Anyway, the horses were wonderful. Jan and Angela
were there plodding around the muddy ring on two
beautiful ones named Mr. Chips and Sky High. Jan said
if you signed up for horseback riding, you got to go
riding in the woods. And you could canter and gallop if
you were good enough. It sounded fine to me.

Dinner was not terrific. I was not happy about it. For
starters, the counselors sat at their own tables. Everyone
else was assigned to a table full of strangers. You could
not eat with your bunkies. This was supposed to encour-
age you to get to know more people. But I did not talk
to anyone during the entire meal, except when the girl
next to me dropped a tomato slice in my lap and apologized as she picked it off my shorts.

"That's O.K.," I said through clenched teeth.

I was embarrassed. I put my fork down and stared at
my plate. Then I looked over at the next table. Mary was
sitting very still. Her hands were in her lap and tears
were running down her cheeks and dripping onto the

table. The girl across from her whispered something to the girl on her right. They glanced at Mary and snickered. I wished I still owned my slingshot.

The other bad thing about dinner was the food. It left a lot to be desired. First we got salad. It was sitting on the tables when we entered the mess hall. I suspected it had been there for several hours. The edges of the lettuce were brown. And little black specks were all over everything. They may have been part of the dressing, but I couldn't be sure. I skipped the salad.

When the rest of our table finished theirs (and I noticed a lot left over), the person at the head took the salad bowl out to the kitchen and brought back a big tray with the main course. Emily had explained that everyone had to be at the head of the table and serve sometimes. You rotated one place to the right at each meal. I counted and realized I would be at the head in five meals—lunch on Tuesday. I planned to have a stomach ache at lunchtime on Tuesday.

The main course was hamburgers and french fries and corn on the cob. Pretty good, Mrs. Wright, I thought. But just to make sure the meat was O.K., I took it out of the bun and cut through the middle. It was pink inside. Just as I had suspected. Pink meat always reminds me of newborn mice. I carefully trimmed around the middle of the hamburger and ate the safe edges.

Dessert was Popsicles. Not the good ice-cream kind, but the slippery, drippy kind that runs down the stick and turns your fingers red and blue. I was very relieved when the meal finally ended and everyone scrambled out the door. I found Emily waiting for me. She had a blue tongue.

We walked together to a clearing where we were going

to have this bonfire and roast marshmallows and sing songs. Honestly. I could do that at home, and Dad and Kate wouldn't have to spend an arm and a leg for it.

At dinner Mrs. Wright had announced that this activity was just something for the Upper Girls. The Lower Girls were going to hear a storyteller.

"Em, what *are* the Upper Girls, anyway?" I asked, trudging along through the underbrush.

"The older girls," she said. "The girls who are ten to fourteen. The Lower Girls are the six- to nine-year-olds."

"Why don't they just call them older and younger girls? 'Lower Girls' sounds like undeveloped plant life."

Emily giggled and shrugged. "I don't know. It's just always been that way, I guess."

The sing-a-long took an hour and a half. It would have ended sooner, but somebody wanted to sing "A Hundred Bottles of Beer on the Wall." Nancy suggested we start at ten.

We started at fifty.

Afterward we somehow found our way back to Misty Mountains. It was pitch-black. Nobody had a flashlight with them. After you've been at Camp Arrowhead awhile, you must develop bat's radar.

We undressed in the dark since the cabins were not equipped with electricity. I crawled into my sleeping bag, zipped it up, and fell asleep instantly.

I woke up at two A.M. and had to go to the bathroom. Very badly. I recalled that we had had hot chocolate at the song fest. And that I had drunk not only mine but Emily's, since she's allergic to chocolate.

Bright, Kammy, I said to myself.

I grabbed my flashlight, dashed outside, and stopped short.

I could not remember how to get to the bathrooms.

I knew there was some sort of path to follow, but I couldn't find it. My flashlight was rather weak. Thanks a lot, Kate. I stuck it in my pocket.

I stood among the trees, surrounded by blackness and silence. It was so dark I could not even see the trees, just sense them.

A stick cracked. I whirled around. Nothing.

I shivered, took a few steps forward, and tripped gracelessly over a tree root. I sat there shaking for a few minutes, then stood up stiffly and groped in front of me. I could feel tears pricking at my eyes, which did not improve my vision any.

By now I had to go to the bathroom so badly my stomach hurt.

"Darn you, Mrs. Wright," I said aloud. And then louder, *"Darn you."* Who ever heard of a bathroom that was miles away from where you lived?

There was nothing else to do. I lifted my nightgown and squatted right where I was. I could feel myself blushing. I had not had to do this since I was two. Even Muffin had not had an accident in all the time I'd known her.

And then the Worst Thing in the World happened.

I heard a door bang. And I heard someone scuffling along toward me. I was nowhere near finished and I could only hope I wasn't making too much noise.

The person was trotting purposefully along about six feet away from me. On the path, no doubt. It was probably Susie. Little Miss Perfect would be able to find the path in a blizzard.

When she was safely by me, I rose slowly and walked in the direction she'd come from. Eventually I bumped into Misty Mountains and by feeling all along the wall, found the door.

I slunk back up to my bunk and lay awake in my sleeping bag. I felt stupid.

If I were at home, Simon would have found me by now. He could tell when I was upset. He would jump on my bed and pad along the blankets until he reached my face. Then he would lick away my tears with his rough little tongue. Thank you, Simon, I would tell him, and cuddle him close.

I burst into tears and cried until I fell asleep.

I looked at my watch. It was five-thirty. We did not have to get up until six-thirty. I reached over to the shelf by my bed for *The Secret Garden*. It was a new book. I had been wanting to read it for ages, and when I'd unpacked my trunk the day before, I'd found it tucked in with my clothes. A note attached to the front said:

> Dear Kammy,
>   This was my favorite book when I was your age. I hope you enjoy it as much as I did.
>   Have lots of fun at camp.
>
> Love,
Kate

It was a very good book. I read for the next hour without stopping. This was not difficult, considering the sun had been shining broadly in the cabin for half an hour already.

I was so caught up in *The Secret Garden* that I forgot all

about the time, and was nearly blasted out of bed when a tinny recording of reveille came blaring over the loud-speaker system.

Nancy woke up immediately. She poked her head through the curtain. "Morning, girls!"

I was the only one who answered.

The other five were sound asleep. How, I don't know. They must have been deaf and blind.

"Come on, everybody," Nancy called.

Emily groaned.

Jan groaned and coughed.

Mary sat up and blinked, looking confused.

Nancy tried again. "You've got half an hour to dress, make up your beds, wash, and be at the mess hall for breakfast."

That did it. Susie went from prone and nearly uncon-scious to upright and bright-eyed in three seconds. She searched through her trunk for clothes. This also took only three seconds. (Her trunk was Organized.)

Slowly everyone else followed her lead.

Except me. I had suddenly grown cold all over. Some-thing awful had occurred to me.

I lay on my stomach in my sleeping bag and looked around at the other girls. They were all getting dressed now. Right out in the open, more or less.

Susie was standing by her bed tugging on her alligator underwear.

Mary was scrabbling around inside her sleeping bag. She kept throwing articles of clothing out—her pajama bottoms, a pair of underpants. I thought she'd found a possible solution until I noticed Jan and Angela pointing at her and giggling.

Both Jan and Angela were in various stages of undress.
They did not seem to care.

There was no way out. I just could not do it. Especially
after I saw Angela make a big production out of putting
on her bra. (Jan put on a training bra. That was not *quite*
such a big production.)

I had no need for a bra yet. Not even a training one.

I peered over my bed to see what Emily was doing. She
was dressing in a corner with her back to everyone. That
absolutely was not a solution. You could see far too
much.

"Twenty minutes," Nancy prodded. "Better hustle.
Kammy, get a move on! What are you doing? I thought
you were up already."

"O.K.," I said faintly.

Susie and Mary headed out the door.

I briefly considered dressing in the bathroom, but that
would mean wandering around camp in my pajamas.

I pulled the sleeping bag over my head and tried not
to cry. I heard Angela and Jan leave.

A voice spoke quietly near my ear.

"Kammy?" It was Emily.

"What?" I was grumpy. I did not feel polite.

"Are you O.K.?"

"Yeah."

"Are you homesick?"

"*No.*"

"You're going to be late."

"Go on without me, O.K.?"

"O.K." I could almost hear her shrug.

The cabin door slammed and everything was quiet.

"Kammy!" Nancy gasped. "You've only got ten minutes."

"Nancy?"

"Yeah?"

"I don't feel too good."

Nancy came over and stood by the bed. She stroked my hair. Dad used to do that when I was sick.

"Where don't you feel good?"

"In my stomach."

"Do you have to throw up?"

"I don't know."

"Maybe you have butterflies. Your first time away from home isn't easy. Have you ever been homesick?"

I shook my head.

Nancy climbed up the ladder and perched on the edge of my bed.

"Is anything bothering you? Anything specific?"

I didn't answer.

"I can't help you if you don't tell me."

"It's embarrassing."

"Try me. I've heard everything." She smiled.

I managed to smile back weakly, the way I do when an eighty-five-year-old relative who hasn't seen me since I was two, informs me I've grown.

There was nothing to do but tell her. "See, I've always had my own room," I began. "Even now, with my new stepsister and stepbrother, I have my own room. And in our locker room at school there are these six changing rooms. I mean, I've never had to get undressed in front of people, and I really can't do it."

"O.K.," said Nancy, "I'll make you a deal. If you can dress really fast, you can change in my room behind the curtain whenever you feel like it."

"What if the other girls make fun of me?"

"You'll have to decide about that, I guess. I mean, you

do have to get dressed. Anyway, maybe the girls won't say anything. You're just assuming they will. But if they do, you can ignore them, or tell them off, or talk to them. I'm afraid I can't do it for you. Why don't you wait and see what happens?"

"O.K."

"I'll dress in my room now," she added, "and you dress out here. I won't come out till you say it's all right." She backed down the ladder. I heard her draw the curtain.

I got up in a hurry and yanked on some clothes.

"Nancy," I called. "I'm ready."

"Go on to the bathrooms and wash up. You'll be a little late when you get to breakfast, but tell Mrs. Wright I said it was O.K. and that I'll talk to her about it when I get there."

"O.K. Bye, Nancy. And thanks." I charged out the door and headed to the mess hall for my first Camp Arrowhead breakfast.

Chapter 7

More Trouble

I don't know how it happened, but somehow I made it through the rest of Monday.

I went on a marathon horseback ride Monday morning. Every new camper who said she had previous riding experience was given a test first thing by the riding counselors. The riding counselors were these identical twins named Sharon and Karen McKeever.

Sharon gave me my test. She asked me to lead Mr. Chips into the ring, mount, and walk him around twice. Then she asked if I could trot and post, then canter, and last of all, gallop. When I finally showed her how I could jump and convinced her I could even saddle a horse, rub him down after a workout, and groom him, she said I definitely belonged in the Advanced Class. This was nice because the Advanced Class was taking a three-hour ride in the woods.

So I was in horse heaven—until I remembered that Tuesday I was supposed to be the server for our table at lunch. I am almost as uncoordinated as my father. I trip a lot and walk into couches and spill things. And they expected *me* to carry heavy trays and pass out dishes and stuff?

I sat back on Mr. Chips and watched the rest of the riders string out in front of me in a neat line.

"Kammy, come on!" In front of me Jan stopped Blue-
bell and turned around to see what I was doing.

I sighed and nudged Mr. Chips with my heels. I let
him walk back to Haven. I just wasn't up to a trot.

After lunch we had a one-hour rest period. It was
called Siesta. But they couldn't fool me. What it was,
was naptime. Like in kindergarten. Everyone had to
stay in her bunk the entire time. It didn't matter what
you did there as long as you stayed put and stayed
quiet. I read *The Secret Garden* for forty-five minutes and
then dashed off a note to Dad. I had to use up those
stamps, after all.

I wrote:

> Dear Father: [I was still mad.]
>
> How are you? I am doing as well as can be
> expected under the circumstances. The bunks
> here are hard as rocks. And the sun comes up
> around 3:30 A.M.
>
> This morning I went on a horseback ride. I
> am in the Advanced Class. I rode Mr. Chips.
>
> Remember that time we ate at Frank's Grill,
> and the next day they condemned the place?
> The food here reminds me quite a bit of the
> food at Frank's.
>
> Tell Kate I like *The Secret Garden* and I'm al-
> ready on page 93.
>
> I hope you're fine and enjoying the nice,
> peaceful summer at home without me.
>
> > Sincerely, your daughter,
> >   Kamilla Whitlock

Just as Siesta was ending, a CIT (Emily told me that
meant "counselor in training") named Jeannie came in

for mail call. She handed out the mail for our cabin (there was not much) and picked up the letters Susie and I had written.

I could not believe it when Jeannie handed me a letter. Camp had just started yesterday.

I looked at the handwriting. I did not recognize it. The postmark was from home, though.

I stared at the handwriting some more and finally tore open the envelope. The notepaper inside said "Kate Whitlock" in little bold letters. She had written it last Thursday before I left.

I stuffed the letter in my trunk.

The rest of the day was so-so. The entire camp was supposed to take swimming tests in the afternoon. They lasted forever. I got out of having to go in the lake by saying I couldn't swim at all. Mrs. Wright was there at the time and I saw her looking at me in a funny way. I wondered if my camp application said what a good swimmer I am.

But there was absolutely no way I was going in that lake.

"Kammy, would you like to wade out just a few feet and see if you can float?" asked Marcia, the swimming counselor.

"No. No, thanks," I said. "It would not be a good idea. I know I can't do it."

I wondered how long I could keep up the charade.

"O.K. We'll start you in the Beginner's Class tomorrow." Marcia made a check mark in her roll book and turned to whisper to Mrs. Wright, while I stood on the edge of the tree-shaded lake and wished I could hear their conversation.

After dinner that night, the Upper Girls got the storyteller and the Lower Girls got the song fest.

We undressed in the dark again. (Whew.)

Nancy let everybody talk for about half an hour after we were in bed. Emily and I used the time to arrange some secret signals we might need to use sometime.

Finally, Nancy called from behind the curtain, "O.K., girls. Quiet down, now."

We all did.

But I could not sleep.

I lay on my side and stretched my toes all the way down till they touched the foot of the bunk. Then I waved my hands around in front of my face, trying to see my fingers. It was impossible. I opened my eyes very wide, but even that did not help.

I listened to the soft night sounds around me: Emily breathing deeply, Susie snoring gently.

I reached into my sleeping bag and pulled out the flashlight. Keeping it carefully covered up, I switched it on without making a sound and got Kate's letter out of my trunk.

Dear Kammy,

It is only Thursday and you haven't even left yet, but I thought you'd like to get a letter right away. I went to camp for one summer when I was ten. My mother made sure I got a letter every day. That made a big difference!

I am writing this with Simon stretched out in my lap imitating big cats. He is sound asleep and his little round tummy is moving up and down. If I touch him he wrinkles his fur but does not wake up!

> Muffin and the baby are both down for naps (thank goodness). It certainly is more peaceful when they're out of commission, isn't it?

I didn't know Kate felt that way about the kids. It was very interesting. I went on reading.

> At the moment you are closed in your bedroom. I am not sure what you're doing. Reading? Knitting?

I had, in fact, been making birthday cards.

> (Did you know that I am a hopeless knitter? A friend of mine tried to teach me when I was eighteen. She gave up. I was a disaster.)

That was the truth.

> Your dad says your grandmother taught you to knit when you were seven and that you've made some beautiful things.

Had he really said that? I wondered what other things they said about me when I was not around. What other *good* things, that is.

> Maybe when you get back you could try to teach me again. Maybe you would be a better teacher than my friend was.
>
> And I could teach *you* something. I know a project that involves art *and* cooking, but I won't tell you what it is until you get home. It will be a surprise. There are so many fun things to do that Muffin is still too little for.

I had to admit that sounded pretty appealing. And it was nice of Kate, I guess.

> That's about all for now. I hope you're enjoy-
> ing camp. The brochures certainly made it look
> like fun.
> I'll be writing again soon.
>
> > Lots of love,
> >
> > Kate
>
> P.S.   The baby, of course, is still nameless. The
> most recent batch of rejections (as you
> may or may not know) includes David,
> Sandy, Paul, Maurice, Walford (my great
> uncle's middle name), and all of chapters
> 5 and 6 in *Name Your Baby*. Got any
> suggestions?

Yes, I thought, but you would probably not care for them.

> P.P.S.   Muffin just woke up. She wants to add
> something to the letter.

The rest of the page was filled with chicken scratches. I have shown Muffin several times how to print a capital *M*, but she never remembers.

I reread the letter twice. It would be fun to teach Kate to knit. *Me* teaching a grownup something! I wondered what Kate's art and cooking project that Muffin couldn't do was.

I was beginning to feel homesick again until I remembered things like colic and Muffin spraying corn flakes across the table. And then, with a jolt, I remembered how badly Kate and Dad wanted me to go to camp. I couldn't figure it out. Did they want me around or not?

I felt like I didn't really belong at camp, or at home, or anywhere.

Tuesday.

Lunch serving day.

I woke up weak-kneed. At four forty-five A.M. An ungodly hour. I hoped the birds were enjoying themselves.

By six-thirty I was almost finished with *The Secret Garden*.

When the reveille thing went off, I leaped out of bed and charged into Nancy's room. I had my underwear and my running shorts and my SAVE AN ALLIGATOR: EAT A PREPPY T-shirt with me.

"Nancy, Nancy!" I gasped. "Let me dress real fast right now. I swear I can do it in less than a minute. You can time me."

So she did and I did.

I was finished before even Susie had gotten out of bed. No one knew. I was safe for another day.

Lunch was at twelve-thirty. Servers were supposed to get there five to ten minutes early to make sure their tables were ready. At twelve-twenty I was, in theory, in the middle of a softball game. In actuality I was sitting somewhere in the outfield looking for four-leaf clovers. I was proceeding under the assumption that nobody could hit a ball as far as I was. This was not true, as a girl named Celeste had proved by hitting several out near me, but Emily, who was in left field and loved softball, kept running over and catching them. A good thing, too, because you have to take off your mitt to look for clovers.

Anyway, at twelve I put my mitt back on and trotted over to Nancy, who was the umpire. I had a plan for getting out of serving at lunch. I ran by her calling over my shoulder, "Gotta go."

"O.K., kiddo," she said, patting me vaguely on the back and staring out into right field where some sort of play was going on.

Very calmly I walked toward the clearing where the mess hall stood. When I was out of sight of the game, I changed direction and ran up to Misty Mountains. I felt like a criminal. But just as if it were the most natural thing to do at twelve twenty-five, I heaved myself onto my bunk and opened up *The Secret Garden.*

I finished it before anything happened and was in the middle of rereading one of the good parts when I heard voices down the hill calling my name.

I ignored them.

The voices got more frantic. Also closer.

"Kammy! Kammy!"

I turned a page.

"Kamilla!"

I thought I could make out Nancy's voice and Karen's and Mrs. Wright's.

"Keep going," Mrs. Wright shouted. "I'll check the cabin."

Our door slammed.

I pretended to be asleep.

"It's O.K.," she called out the door in a few seconds.

"Kamilla Whitlock." In those two words Mrs. Wright spoke an entire paragraph. It was one of those parent paragraphs with things like "What on earth are you doing here? You had us so worried. I don't know whether to laugh or cry." (Or hug you or turn you over my knee—there are several variations.) "I know you're not asleep, so you can quit faking it. I want you to sit up right now and face the music. I think I deserve an explanation."

I sat up. I faced the music.

"Mrs. Wright, I can explain this," I said.

"O.K."

That was it. That was all she said. A very cold "O.K." It was the third word she had spoken since she entered Misty Mountains.

"Well, see—"

"The truth, Kamilla."

Mrs. Wright's face was the color of chalk. She was tight-lipped. I was pretty sure those were two danger signs.

I sighed heavily. "I was standing out in the hot sun playing softball and suddenly I began to feel faint—"

"Nancy said you looked fine when you left and didn't say anything about feeling ill."

I blushed. How was I going to get out of this one? "I didn't want to worry her?" I suggested.

"Well, did you or didn't you want to worry her?" asked Mrs. Wright quietly.

I scowled down at my hands. I really hadn't meant to cause trouble. I just didn't want to be the server. I wondered if I should tell her that, but she started talking again.

"You've been here just two days, and I feel it is only fair to give you a chance to get your bearings." She paused for a minute and looked a little less angry. "Are you homesick?" she asked finally.

"I don't know."

"Well, I'm always available if you want to talk."

"O.K."

"You can stay here until Siesta starts. But from now on I expect you to show up at every meal and every one of your activities, O.K.?"

"O.K."

Mrs. Wright patted me on the head and left. I do not pat people on the head, because that is what you do to dogs. I do not even pat Muffin on the head.

I leaned back against the wall and waited for Siesta.

CHAPTER 8

The Case of the Missing Clothes

I stood on the sandy shore of Lake Oconomowoc. I was wearing my new Speedo suit. The one with red palm trees all over it.

A bunch of kids were splashing around in the lake several feet away. Some were swimming. Some were wading. They all looked happy. They looked like kids who would have their pictures taken for the Camp Arrowhead pamphlet to show how much fun it is to swim in Lake Oconomowoc.

I kept scanning the water for long, dark shapes. When I finally saw one, I inhaled for a healthy scream before I realized the shape belonged to a stick. I let out my breath in a trembling sigh. Even if someone were to drain the whole lake and show me that no snakes were left behind, I wouldn't go in when it was filled up again. A snake could always fall out of a tree, or slither in accidentally—and you would never know it until that snake was wrapping itself around you . . .

Something touched my bare shoulder.

I gasped and jumped.

"Oh, Marcia," I cried. I sounded hysterical. "You startled me."

"I'm sorry. I didn't mean to, honey. Listen, the beginning group is meeting over there." She pointed to a crowd of Lower Girls, most of whom were about six or seven years old, all standing in shallow water at one end of the "beach."

"O.K."

"So grab your towel and come on over." Marcia smiled. She had pretty brown eyes. I wanted her to like me, but not if it meant risking snakes.

"Oh, I . . . I left my towel in the beachhouse. I'll be right there."

I really had left my towel in the beachhouse. (On purpose, of course, but why split hairs?) It was in one of the changing rooms. I walked back as slowly as I could, pausing in the doorway to see what Marcia was doing with the Lower Girls. They had their faces in the water and were blowing bubbles.

I took my time getting the towel. As I was leaving, I heard someone behind me and looked back over my shoulder.

"Hi, Kammy," said Susie cheerfully.

I was surprised to see her there, since it meant she was late for her lesson. And Miss Susie Goody-Two-Shoes Benson was always On Time, according to Emily.

"Hi," I said.

"What group are you in?" she asked as we headed back to the sand.

"Oh, that one," I said pointing in the general direction of the end of the beach.

It did not fool Susie.

"The *baby* group?" She was incredulous. "You're kidding. You can't *swim?*" She snickered. "What a baby. You won't undress in front of anyone, you can't swim, you don't even know enough to go to meals."

"Shut up," I hissed. "Who do you think you are? Miss Perfection?"

"Miss Perfection! Ha ha. You don't know names yet either."

"I do, too, Susan Benson. And I'd like to know why *you* are late for swimming, if you are so great."

We were squared off, each armed with a towel. I wished mine were wet enough to whip her a good rat tail.

"If it's so important to *you*," Susie sputtered, "you might as well know I was getting Nancy's towel for her. She left it behind and asked *me* to get it." Susie was smirking.

"Well, if you *like* being a slave . . ." I said calmly, and left both the sentence and Susie's mouth hanging as I stalked over to Marcia.

Susie was going to get it.

I managed not to go in the water during the whole lesson. Marcia was so busy keeping track of the other kids (six-year-olds run around a lot) that she hardly noticed me. When we had to wait on line to do things one at a time, I just kept moving to the back. The Lower Girls didn't notice, and Nancy always had her hands full with whomever she was teaching.

At one point, when we were all strung out along the shore, Marcia yelled, "O.K., Kammy, your turn!" I shoved little Patsy McClure in front of me and yelled, "No, I think Patsy's next." Patsy dashed gaily off to Marcia and I breathed a sigh of relief.

It was just a few minutes later when I noticed Mrs. Wright standing in the door of the beachhouse. She was staring at me. I expected her to come barreling down to the Beginners and demand to know why my suit was dry. But she didn't, even though I was becoming more and more convinced my application said I was a good swimmer. Camp directors always ask for that kind of information, don't they?

Mrs. Wright reminded me of the Wicked Witch of the West, biding her time. I wondered when she would strike.

As soon as the whistle blew signaling the end of lessons, I tore over to the Advanced group and pulled Emily away by the arm.

"Hey!" she cried.

"Ssh," I said, and dragged her all the way to the beachhouse, giving her a fast rundown on what Susie had said earlier.

"That little rat!" exploded Emily.

"Want to help me play a trick on her?" I asked.

"Anything," said Emily, grinning devilishly. "She did some real stinky things to me last summer."

"All right. Get changed as fast as you can and meet me right outside the door."

I was in and out of my clothes and standing by the beachhouse in a flash. The other campers were streaming past me now, heading in to change and shower. I gazed out over the beach and caught sight of Susie helping Nancy collect kickboards and goggles and flippers. The little swine.

"She'll learn," I said under my breath.

Emily joined me. I pointed Susie out to her and quickly explained what we were going to do.

Five minutes later Susie finally gave up her maid duties and started for the beachhouse. A lot of the campers had left by then, but plenty were still dressing. Emily and I pretended to be engaged in conversation as Susie walked by us.

"Are you sure she always showers?" I whispered when she was out of earshot.

"Positive," Emily whispered back. "She's perfect, remember?"

We peeked around into the beachhouse just in time to see Susie deposit her beautifully folded and cared-for alligator clothes on a stool outside the shower. Soon she tossed her nearly dry bathing suit on the pile. When we heard the water go on, Emily nonchalantly picked up all of Susie's clothes, including her bathing suit, and ran them back to Misty Mountains.

Then it was just a matter of waiting. I milled around with the fifteen or so other kids until we heard a shout.

"Hey!"

The beachhouse grew quiet.

"Hey!" Susie yelled again, from the shower stall.

"What?" someone asked. "Is something wrong?"

"Yes, something is wrong. My clothes are gone!"

"Gone!" I cried. "You don't mean it. Susie, is that you?"

"Of course it is, and I can tell that's you, Kammy, and if you took my clothes I'll kill you!"

"*Me?* Why would I take your clothes? I don't even like them. For goodness' sake, everybody spread out and start looking."

Emily arrived breathlessly back at the beachhouse just as all the girls began searching through the dressing rooms, under benches, and in their own duffel bags. She joined the search with a straight face.

Periodically, Susie's arm would reach out the door to

the shower stall and feel around on the stool to see if her
clothes had magically reappeared. And each time she felt
the empty stool, she'd yell some more. Things like
"Come on, I'm freezing! Those were my best clothes. I'll
get whoever did this." And finally she just started sort of
screaming in general.

In the middle of all the pandemonium, Mrs. Wright,
Marcia, and Nancy walked in.

Mrs. Wright clapped her hands twice.

Silence.

"What is going on in here?" she asked.

Susie started up again. "My clothes are gone," she
wailed. "Someone *took* them. Everyone is so mean. I'm
freezing!"

"Calm down, Susie," said Mrs. Wright.

Nancy tossed a couple of extra towels in to her.

"Does anybody know where Susie's clothes are?" Mrs.
Wright asked.

"I don't think so," I said. "That's why we've been
looking for them for the last ten minutes."

Mrs. Wright narrowed her eyes at me.

"Susie," she went on, crossing to the shower and yelling over the stall, "do you have any idea what happened
to your clothes?"

"Kammy took them," Susie answered promptly.

"Are you sure? Did you see her take them?"

"Well, no . . . but I know she did. She's such a baby."

"That's enough, Susie. Kamilla, what do you have to
say about this?"

"I don't know where her clothes are. I was just in here
changing and suddenly Susie started screaming about
her clothes."

Emily cleared her throat. "Um, excuse me. I wasn't here or anything when it happened, but . . ." She paused as if she were too nervous to go on.

"Yes, Emily?" coaxed Mrs. Wright.

Emily lowered her eyes to the floor. "Well, I don't want to embarrass Susie," she whispered, "but remember last year when she couldn't find her clothes after swimming and it turned out she had changed in the cabin instead of the beachhouse, and left her clothes there?"

"No . . . I'm not sure I do remember," said Mrs. Wright slowly.

"That's because it never happened," shouted Susie. "She's lying."

Emily let her lower lip quiver just enough to be noticeable, and hung her head.

"That's all right, dear," soothed Mrs. Wright. "Memories can be tricky. Even if it didn't happen, it's a good suggestion about what might have happened today. Susie, are you sure you changed here?"

"*Yes.* How could I forget? Anyway, I never change in the cabin."

"Mrs. Wright," I said meekly, stepping forward, "I— I could go up to the cabin and—and just, you know, check. I wouldn't mind. Really."

"Well, Kammy, that would be very kind of you. That's a nice offer."

I ran to Misty Mountains and back in record time. Emily had dumped the whole pile of clothes on Susie's bunk, so I gathered it up and presented it proudly to Mrs. Wright.

"The problem is solved," I announced grandly.

"Thank you very much, Kammy." Mrs. Wright beamed at me. "Here you go, Susie," she said.

The door to the shower stall opened up about two inches. Susie stuck her arm out and snatched in the clothes. She didn't say a word.

A few minutes later Emily and I were laughing hysterically and dancing around outside. We were patting ourselves on the back for fooling Susie.

Suddenly a triumphant "Aha!" was shouted from the beachhouse.

Susie.

Emily and I looked at each other warily.

"I think we better get out of here," Emily whispered.

But we didn't have time.

"Kamilla and Emily. Would you please come inside for a moment?"

Mrs. Wright faced us in the beachhouse. She was holding Susie's bathing suit. "If Susie changed in the cabin," she said, "I would like to know how she managed to leave her bathing suit there with her clothes and then come to the lake for swimming lessons. I don't recall seeing anyone running nude through camp."

"She created an illusion?" I suggested.

Mrs. Wright sighed. I sighed. Emily sighed. I remembered that I used to make Kate sigh.

"You two may help wash the dishes after supper tonight," pronounced Mrs. Wright. "And Kamilla," she added, leading me out of the beachhouse, away from the others, "I want you to come with me to the office. We're going to call your parents so we can discuss this incident, as well as your disappearance at lunch, with them."

Call home! I was already on Dad's and Kate's bad sides after my behavior over coming to Camp Arrowhead. What would they think now? I couldn't decide if the phone call was a good or bad idea. Maybe they'd see the error of their ways and let me come home. But did I want that?

Finally I just said, "I don't know if you'll be able to reach them. It's Tuesday. They're both probably at the university. Summer session started yesterday."

"Both your parents work?" Mrs. Wright asked.

I could see the wheels turning. *Lonely, neglected child of working parents. Obvious adjustment problems.*

"Yes, my father and stepmother work." I enunciated each word carefully to make sure she got the point. About who Kate was, that is.

The wheels turned a bit further. *Member of broken family.*

"Then we'll try calling them tonight," she said.

She turned on her heel and left me standing by the beachhouse.

CHAPTER 9

Ups and Downs

Thanks to Susie and her big mouth, Emily and I had not been able to leave the kitchen until seven forty-five, over an hour after supper ended. One hundred kids and counselors sure do use a lot of dishes and things. My fingers looked like prunes by the time the cook said we could go.

Emily and I burst out of the building. We were missing a rousing campwide game of Capture the Flag. I could see Emily getting anxious to play. I, personally, did not care which side ended up with the flag and got the ice cream. So I was only slightly upset when Mrs. Wright snagged me and suggested that now would be a nice, quiet time to use the office phone.

Emily ran off to war, and I trailed Mrs. Wright into the office. She motioned me to another little room. I sat down on a couch and looked for a telephone. I did not see one.

Mrs. Wright sat next to me. "Kammy, if you don't mind," she said, "I'd like to speak to your parents first —in private. Then you may speak to them in private. Is that all right with you?"

I nodded.

"Also, I want you to understand that calling your parents is not a punishment. I simply want them to be aware of what is happening here. Maybe they can help. And maybe you'll feel better after you've spoken to them."

I didn't know if I was supposed to say anything, so I just nodded again.

Mrs. Wright got up and closed the door between me and the office.

I jumped up and put my ear to the door, but I couldn't hear much. Just some low murmurings. Mrs. Wright had either a very soft phone voice or a very thick door.

I sat back down and thumbed through a copy of *Highlights for Children.* It is a magazine I happen to hate because the only other place I ever see it is the dentist's office.

After about five minutes the door opened and I went in and sat behind Mrs. Wright's desk. She ducked into the other room and closed the door. I wondered if she was standing plastered against the crack trying to overhear *me*.

I picked up the phone. "Hello?"

"Hello! Hello!" Two hearty hellos from Dad and Kate. They were each on an extension.

"What's up, pumpkin?" asked Dad. "Mrs. Wright told us about today, but I want to hear your side."

"Why, nothing, Dad," I said. "You and Kate said this would be a terrific place for me, and it sure is. You sure were right."

"That sounds a bit sarcastic, Kammy," Dad said quietly.

I did not answer him. There was this huge silence.

"Kammy?"

"Yes?"

"Mrs. Wright says there's been a bit of trouble today."

"Mrs. Wright is a st—" I broke off. I was going to call her a stinker, but that is not one of Dad's favorite words. "Mrs. Wright doesn't know how to run a camp."

I heard a sort of muffled choking sound on Dad's end of the phone. He had a hard time concealing a laugh.

"Really, Dad," I insisted. "She runs a stupid camp. She serves disgusting food and puts the bathrooms out where you can't find them and there's no electricity in the cabins and no place to change your clothes, and that made me late to breakfast the first morning because"— I could feel my face burning—"I didn't want to undress in front of the other girls." The last couple of words came out sounding kind of choked.

"Oh," said Kate slowly. "I see. Robert, would you mind hanging up? I think I hear the baby fussing. I'll call you back to the phone in just a moment."

"Yes, O.K.," said Dad hastily.

"Kams?"

"Yeah?" I hardly even noticed that Kate had used my father's special nickname for me.

"How come you don't like to undress in front of the others?"

I breathed in a long, shaky breath. "It's hard to explain."

"I was wondering if it might have something to do with wearing a bra."

"Well . . ."

"You know what? I didn't need my first bra until I was thirteen, but my sister, who is two years younger than I am, needed *her* first bra the same day I did! I was pretty mad at her, but my mother pointed out that everyone grows differently. And in the long run it won't matter much what size you are—or whether you have brown hair or blond hair, or green eyes or brown eyes, or you're five foot four or five foot eight. It's what's inside that counts. You've probably heard that all before and it probably doesn't mean much, but just file it away for later. And remember that your friends are not going to like you for your chest size."

I tried to get control of my voice. Maybe it would not be so bad to have a mother again. "Kate?" I finally said.

"What, sweetie?"

"Thanks a lot for your letter. It was really nice. And I promise to teach you to knit when I get home. I bet I can do it."

"I bet you can, too."

"And I've got a suggestion for the baby's name."

"Oh, good. What?"

"Benjamin Alexander Dumas."

"You don't think it's a little long?"

I giggled.

Kate giggled, too. "I'll keep it in mind. How do you feel about Ferdinand?"

"Yuck."

"My sentiments exactly. It was your father's suggestion. I couldn't tell if he was kidding."

"He was kidding," I said.

"Let me get him back on. . . . Rob? Rob?" I heard her yell.

Dad picked up. "Is the girl talk over?" he asked slyly.

"Oh, Dad." I laughed.

"Kams, I'd really like to end this conversation right

now while we're all so jolly, but Mrs. Wright did take the trouble to call and I want to hear what you have to say about the things that happened today."

"Oh, all right. I did miss lunch today. I just didn't feel like going. And they thought I was lost."

"In a place like camp or school you can't do that, though," said Dad. "Mrs. Wright is responsible for you. Can you imagine how she must have felt when she thought one of her campers was lost?"

I was having an easier time remembering how I felt when I was too scared to serve lunch, but I wasn't going to bring that up. I'd already brought up the business of not wanting to get undressed. And I didn't want Dad or Kate thinking I was a baby. Because I wasn't. I really wasn't. No matter what Susie said.

"What happened at your swimming lessons?" asked Kate.

"It was just a joke."

"It didn't sound very nice," said Dad thoughtfully. "How do you think the other girl felt?"

"I don't care." I knew I sounded whiny. "She was mean to me first. I was just giving her what she deserved. Besides, it was kind of funny."

"It just doesn't sound like you," said my father.

Then maybe you don't know me anymore, I thought.

"Dad, you weren't there. You don't know Susie. You don't know what it's like at Camp Arrowhead," I said.

I heard Dad and Kate sigh. I was making people sigh again.

"Look," my father said finally, "would you please try to behave yourself? I'm not sure what you're up to, but just try to shape up a little, O.K.?"

I couldn't promise because I wasn't going to shape up. I still had to find ways to get out of serving and swimming lessons and who knew what else. I settled on saying (very contritely), "I'll try to change." I hoped that covered all bases—I did not say *how* I would change.

"Good," Dad and Kate said together.

"That's very cute," I said.

"What is?"

"The way you two have learned to speak in unison." A month ago I would have been mad about it. Now I thought it was funny. And something about being on the telephone made talking easier.

Dad chuckled. "I guess we're getting used to each other."

"Used to each other!" cried Kate. "I hope it hasn't come to that!"

The conversation ended that way, with the three of us kind of joking and teasing. "See you in eleven days," I said. I was smiling when I hung up the phone.

In fact, I was feeling so much better that after a little chat with Mrs. W (in which I finally promised to be a better Arrowhead camper), I ran up the hill to where Capture the Flag was still raging. I caught sight of Emily, Jan, and Angela sneaking around in a tight pack.

"Come help us!" hissed Jan. "We're about to storm the headquarters!"

This time, I didn't hold back. I joined right in. We were just in sight of the flag. Only two girls were guarding it. Jan threw a stone in the bushes behind them. It landed with a satisfying thud and crackle. When they turned to see who was sneaking up on them, we grabbed the flag and tore back to our side.

"The winners! The winners!" Our team, Upper and Lower Girls alike, was jumping up and down and yelling. Emily and Jan and Angela and I all hugged each other. And when the ice cream came, I found I was starved.

Later my bunkies and I walked back to Misty Mountains together. We were marching along in pairs with our arms around each other, and Angela started singing, "Oh, You Can't Get to Heaven." We all joined in. Even me. For once, someone had chosen a decent song.

That night we were so keyed up that Nancy let us talk longer than usual. Just after she gave us one more ten-more-minutes signal, Jan called out, "Jumping practice tomorrow, Kammy. Are you going to be there?"

"Sure," I said. Jumping was one thing I particularly liked.

"And arts and crafts begins tomorrow," announced Angela. "Who's going to be there?"

"I am," Mary and I called out together. I couldn't wait to get inside of Sunny Skies again.

In a few minutes Nancy gave us the final signal.

I fell asleep barely noticing that Susie had not said a word all evening.

Wednesday was mostly terrific.

It started off when I realized that, as long as I was waking up so early anyway, I could change my clothes in my sleeping bag and no one would know. By the time everyone else woke up, I was sitting on my bunk reading, fully dressed.

The next good thing was my first arts and crafts class. I wallowed in Sunny Skies for over two and a half hours. Mary spent the morning with me. It turned out she liked art as much as I did.

"What are you going to work on?" I asked her.

Janine, the art counselor, had just finished showing us where everything was and explaining how some of the equipment worked.

"I think I'll do a mosaic," she answered, smiling. "This cabin is great, isn't it? I can't believe all the stuff they've got here. What are you going to make?"

I had never heard Mary say so much at once. She positively glowed.

I smiled back at her. "I really wanted to use the pottery wheels, but now I don't know. I saw all those scraps of fabric. Maybe I'll make a patchwork quilt."

"Oh, that's a good idea! Except a quilt's so big."

"I know. That's why I was thinking I could make a little quilt for Simon. He's my cat. And then I thought I could even make a quilt for my—my stepbrother. He's just a baby. I think he'd like a quilt. Except Kate, my stepmother, has bought him all this beautiful stuff from stores. Maybe she wouldn't want something homemade for him."

"I bet she would," cried Mary. "Listen, you could make a really fantastic quilt. Better than anything you'd find in a store."

"Yeah," I said softly. "I could appliqué animals on it."

"And sew on snaps and buttons and zippers so he could learn to dress himself."

"Yeah!" I'd make the best quilt Kate had ever seen. I could really show her I was special. In fact, I could make something for everyone. Presents for everyone, to say, "I didn't mean to be such a pill."

Mary and I spent the rest of the morning searching through piles of tiles and fabric, finding what we needed to start our projects. I could not wait to come back Friday morning.

During Siesta I got two letters—one from Dad and one from Muffin. I opened Dad's first.

> Dear Kammy,
>   It's that hour of night you and I always enjoy. The darkness has just fallen and I am sitting on the back porch, with the kerosene lamp burning, listening to the crickets chirp and the birds settle down for a few hours.

A few hours is right. I should know.

>   I can hear Simon prowling around outside. He has not learned to be quiet yet. He's got a long way to go before he could sneak up on something. Maybe that's just as well for the mice and birds.

Mice, yes. Birds, I would have to think about.

Dad went on a while longer about Simon and the birds and the nighttime. He has a real imagination. Why he is an economics professor and not an English professor or a writer, I'll never know.

He didn't mention camp, which was typical. It's hard for him to bring up unpleasant things. He'd rather ignore them.

I sprawled on my bunk, feeling lazy and enjoying his

letter and wanting very much to go home so I could sit on the porch with him. I'd like to curl up on the deck chairs with Simon beside me, kneading his soft paws in my shorts, and talk to Dad about books and people and the news.

Then I got to the last paragraph of the letter.

> Saturday is Muffin's fourth birthday. She's been asking for a party. Kate feels she can't manage a big one right after the wedding and the move. So she and Muffin and Mrs. Meade have settled on throwing a smaller party—just ten of Muffin's closest nursery school pals—in the afternoon. Then Kate and I will take her to dinner at McDonald's and over to Pennington to see the Hunt Brothers' Circus.

The little brat! I crumpled the letter in a tight ball and shoved it down behind a box of Kleenex on my shelf. How did *she* rate a party? No one ever offered me a party on my birthday. Birthdays had always been special days, like Thanksgiving, that Dad and I spent together. But no parties since Mom died. And now Muffin rates a party *and* dinner *and* the circus? Incredible. It was disgusting. Dad and Kate lavishing all that attention on her while I got shoved out the door and into Camp Arrowhead.

I curled up in a miserable lump, stuck Muffin's unopened letter under my pillow, and waited for Siesta to be over. I tried very hard not to cry, but a couple of stray tears escaped anyway.

They did not go unnoticed.

"Baby, baby, baby," I heard Susie sing softly.

I glanced over at her. It was hard to believe she was breaking the Silence Rule. She must really have it in for me. She'd never call Mary a baby.

She saw me looking at her. "Baby, baby, baby," she sang again.

"You wait, Susan Benson," I spat. "Just wait."

CHAPTER 10

Three-Fingered Willie

It was a good thing I was going horseback riding that afternoon, since Susie cannot ride worth beans, so she'd be out of my hair for once. Also because being around horses always cheers me up.

Jan and I and four other girls went to the jumping ring and worked out with Karen for a couple of hours before we decided to go galloping in the horse pasture. I bumped along on Mr. Chips with my hair flying in the wind. Jan began yahooing and roping imaginary cows, and soon we were all laughing and pretending to be cowgirls.

Finally we slowed down. I walked Mr. Chips around a quiet end of the pasture, and my mind began to wander. That was when I remembered this really gruesome horror story called "Three-Fingered Willie." In fourth grade I told it better than anyone else. I would not want to let my reputation slip. I decided I should tell the story here—and then our cabin could find out just who the biggest baby really was, me or Susie.

I would have to wait until the counselors were not around if I was going to do justice to "Three-Fingered Willie." I got my chance Thursday evening.

After dinner the Upper Girls held this Festival of Owatonna (Omatomma? Owertanna? I never heard it the same way twice) during which we paddled around Lake Oconomowoc in canoes decorated with lighted candles and then got off on this little island and roasted marshmallows. I was never clear who Owentenna was or what we were celebrating. Anyway, the whole thing was only designed to make us all tired enough so we'd go back to our cabins and sleep while the counselors and Mrs. Wright held a meeting in the mess hall.

On the walk back to Misty Mountains I told Em about old Willie. Since she was still feeling pretty chilly toward Susie because of the dishwashing we'd had to do, she was more than ready to help out with the story.

I waited until we were all in bed and Nancy had left for the meeting. I let her get about five steps away before I whispered, "Does anybody want to hear a horror story?"

"Oh, yes!" squealed Jan and Angela and Emily and Mary. Susie was not speaking to me.

"O.K., to make it really scary, put your sleeping bags on the floor and we'll sit together in the middle of the cabin."

In two minutes everyone but Susie was settled in a tight knot.

"Come on, Susie," said Mary. "You have to come, too, or it won't be any good."

"It won't be any good anyway," Susie said under her breath, but she dragged herself over to the group all the same.

"Everyone, put out your flashlights," I instructed. "This has to be told in the absolute dark." The flashlights went off. Our cabin was silent.

"About twenty years ago," I began, "way out in the woods in Connecticut—"

"In Connecticut?" squeaked Angela. "Is this a true story, Kammy?"

"It's supposed to be. You can't be sure about horror stories, but this one was told to me by somebody very reliable who doesn't make things up."

"Where in Connecticut?" interrupted Angela again.

"Outside Ridgefield, I think."

Finally I got a reaction out of Susie.

"Ridgefield! That's right near here!"

"Yes," I said. "Anyway, way out in the woods was this dreadful old cabin. It was all dirty and falling apart. There was old dried food all over the stove, and dirty rags on the beds instead of blankets, and just logs for chairs. And it snowed all winter.

"And in the cabin lived a very mean man, Old Joe, and a little boy, Willie. When he was just a baby, Willie was left on Old Joe's doorstep by some gypsies. Old Joe was a crazy hermit, so he didn't really want a baby, but he thought maybe the boy would be able to help out around the cabin.

"So Old Joe made Willie into his slave. He made him do all the work in the cabin. And all winter he made him stand out in the snow with no coat or gloves and chop firewood.

"Well, the years passed and Willie got to be eighteen years old. He grew very tall and strong—as strong as three men—from all the chopping and work he did. Then one day in February he was standing outside in the snow, chopping wood as usual, when"—I lowered my voice dramatically—"it *happened.*"

"What happened?" cried Jan.

"Willie lowered his ax and—BANG!"—I clapped my hands together and scared everybody to death—"He chopped off the thumb and first finger on his right hand!"

"Oh, dis*gust*ing!" screamed Emily.

"Yeah," I said. "At first he didn't even know because his hands were so frozen he couldn't feel anything, but then he saw red snow at his feet. When he realized what he had done, he started hollering and dancing around. He pounded into the cabin screaming, 'Joe, Joe, my hand, my hand!' but Joe was asleep and would not wake up.

"So Willie just went berserk. He took his ax and chopped up Old Joe. And *then*," I whispered, "he went back out to the chopping block and found his thumb and finger and strung them on a piece of rope. He put that rope around his neck . . . and he never took it off."

"Eeeeeeyew!" squealed Susie. I had her full attention.

Meanwhile, Emily, who was sitting nearest the door, kept inching closer to it. Nobody noticed.

"Well, two years went by," I continued, "and nobody heard from Willie. Except for a couple of farmers who claimed he roamed around the woods completely crazy. He grew fur over his entire body and fangs as sharp as ice picks, and his pupils disappeared! He just had two naked white eyes. When he got hungry he'd—BOOM!"—everyone shrieked again—"reach out and yank a sheep or calf off a farm and eat it without even cooking it."

"Ooh. Ooh. Gross."

"And then," I hissed, "somebody did hear from Willie.

Two very unfortunate people. Two high school girls named Becky and Marty. They were camping out in the woods in a big tent. At about two o'clock in the morning they were awakened by the sound of leaves crunching nearby."

I took a candy wrapper out of my sleeping bag and crumpled it loudly. Susie jumped. Mary cried out and, sounding like she was near tears, quavered, "What happened, Kammy?"

In all the confusion, Emily slipped outside. I went on with the story.

"Then the girls heard an odd voice. It was deep and growly—sort of the way you'd expect a . . . wolf . . . to sound. And they heard fingernails scratching on their tent. The voice didn't say many real words. Mostly it rambled on in gibberish. But sometimes it would call out the girls' names. 'Beckeeee, Marteeee.' Finally it just started screaming.

"The girls were scared stiff. They sat in their tent and watched the shadow of Willie outside. They were afraid to leave and they were afraid to stay. They thought maybe if they kept quiet he would run off. But he didn't. The next thing they knew he came crashing through their tent—and strangled both of them.

"A couple of days later," I went on sadly, "two forest rangers found the girls. At first they could not figure out how they had died. Then they looked at their necks and saw the marks of three fingers . . . and knew Three-Fingered Willie had been there."

"Oooh," shivered Angela, "that's sooo scary."

"I know," I whispered. "Unfortunately, it's not the end of the story."

"It's not?"

"No. A few days later, at a summer camp called Camp Parsipanee" (somebody drew in her breath sharply and squeaked, "That's right down the road!"), "five boys and their counselor who had been on an overnight camping trip were found dead in the woods. *Each one had the mark of three fingers on his neck.*

"After that, Willie would kill about once every month or so. No one ever knew where he would strike next." I stopped to catch my breath, and a faint scratching sound was heard.

"Kammy, stop it, you've scared us to death already," moaned Susie.

"Stop what? I'm not doing anything."

"But don't you hear that?"

Everybody stopped talking. Nobody even breathed. The scratching began again.

"Oh, what *is* that?" cried Mary. "It sounds like it's outside. Didn't you say Willie scratched on Becky and Marty's tent before—before he . . . ?"

The scratching stopped. We all sat in the pitch-black and nighttime silence and began to breathe sighs of relief. Then the wailing began. Emily was doing an awfully good job.

"Oooooeeeeeee ooowaaaaa. Eeeeaghhhh. Ooooosuu-uuu. Oooooosuuuuu. Suseeeeee. *Suseeeee.*"

"Aghh!" yelled Susie. "He's calling my name! He's calling my name!"

Suddenly everyone was screaming and shouting and running around.

"Help! Help me!" That was Susie again. She felt she was in more danger than the rest of us.

Someone flicked on a flashlight. To my relief, Emily was back inside.

"Help!" screamed Susie even louder than before. She sounded slightly hysterical.

"Shhh," I hissed at her. "Everyone be quiet."

Everyone calmed down. Silence.

"But I know he's out there! He's still after me. He's just waiting until I go outside. Help! Help!"

Outside a stick cracked. I almost screamed myself. Everyone else went crazy.

"Help! Help!"

"Save us!"

"Aughh!"

Suddenly the room was flooded with light.

"Girls! What's wrong?"

It was Nancy and Mrs. Wright with a flashlight as bright as a couple of headlights.

Susie positively flung herself on Nancy.

"He's out there! He's out there! Three-Fingered Willie! He's after me. He was calling my name. I thought he was going to kill me." Susie was sobbing for real. I actually felt slightly sorry for her.

After Nancy quieted her down, Mrs. Wright asked her what happened.

"Kammy was telling us a horror story, Mrs. Wright. It was awful. She scared us out of our wits. And then when the story was over we heard someone outside scratching on our cabin and calling my name, just like in the story."

Nancy and Mrs. Wright glanced at each other.

"And do you really believe Three-Fingered Willie was out there, Susie?" asked Mrs. Wright.

"N-no. I guess not. . . . I bet it was a trick! *She* tricked me. She tricked me again, Mrs. Wright!"

I stuck out my tongue at Susie. Mrs. Wright caught me.

"Kamilla," she said. Her voice was sharp enough to dice celery. "I'll tell the cook that you'll be helping out in the kitchen after dinner for the next five evenings. Furthermore, one more incident, one more bit of trouble from you, and I will have to take serious action of some sort."

I opened my mouth. "No questions," snapped Mrs. Wright. "Everybody in bed now. It's late."

It took almost an hour for us to settle down in our bunks. When things were finally quiet, I reached under my pillow and drew out Muffin's letter. I scrunched all the way down inside my sleeping bag and turned on the weak flashlight. What kind of letter could Muffin possibly send?

I slit the envelope and pulled out a piece of pink construction paper folded about twenty-four times. I tried to smooth it out. On it Muffin had drawn a wobbly picture of a girl. Next to it was a big 4 and a big *M*. So she had learned to write the *M* after all. I was possibly the only living being who knew that Muffin's "letter" meant "Muffin is excited about her fourth birthday." And she wanted me to know! It was sort of cute. But it was hard to tell if she was writing because she liked me or if this was just a thinly disguised reminder to send her a birthday present.

I pushed away the whole problem and fell asleep, alternately smiling over the story of Three-Fingered Willie and worrying over what sort of action Mrs. Wright might take.

And I decided to pretend that Susie Benson was not alive.

CHAPTER 11

More Ups and Downs

On Saturday morning something sort of interesting happened. I went to a drama workshop and liked it.

The only reason I had signed up for drama was to stay out of this nature study group that had to tramp around in the woods collecting live specimens that later would be speared onto display cases.

But drama turned out to be a lot of fun. Angela and I walked over together. She had signed up for the same reason I had.

"It's gross," she said. "Do you know how they kill the frogs before they dissect them? They *pith* them. They take this long needle—"

"Stop!" I shrieked. "I don't want to know."

"I wish we could spend every day in the arts and crafts room."

"Me, too," I said wistfully.

"But I guess we have to let other people have a turn. Like *Susie.*"

I looked at her sharply.

"Have you *seen* what she's making?" Angela asked. "It's so *stupid.* But, then, we have to remember Susie's special problems."

Her special problems? I had been tormenting a handicapped person? I cringed. "What problems?" I whispered.

"It's very sad. Susie was born without an imagination or a sense of humor."

I laughed. It was more a laugh of relief than a laugh of humor. I was beginning to feel just the teeniest bit sorry for Susie. Nobody really liked her.

The first thing we did in the drama class was "loosen up," shake out our bodies, and scream! It was weird, but fun. After we were loosened, we all settled down in a clearing in the woods. Cassandra, our drama coach, said our first project would be to prepare a short play to present to the parents on Visiting Day. I had never been in a play, but it sounded like fun. By the time the morning was over we had written the play, and I volunteered to work on painting scenery, *and* got a bit part as the grandmother. Imagine me in a play! I wondered if I would get stage fright. I wondered if stage fright felt the same as homesickness.

At noon we broke for lunch and I walked to the mess hall alone, feeling rather proud of myself for knowing how to get there. A few things were coming more easily now; like I had found my way to the bathroom in the dark a couple of times, and I knew my way all around camp. Swimming and undressing and serving were still problems, but I wasn't worrying about them just then. I bounced along in the warm sunshine, whistling and thinking about the quilt I was making.

The last thing I expected to see was a foot shooting across the path. I didn't exactly sprawl on the ground, but I came close. I thanked my lucky stars for a little tree branch that was within grabbing distance.

The foot belonged to Susie. She was smirking again.

"Jerk," I said hotly, without thinking. It is hard to

pretend someone does not exist when that person has just made a fool of you.

"Baby," she said as she ran off down the path, turning around long enough to stick out her tongue at me.

Angela was right. Susie did not have much of an imagination. She had called me names about eleven times so far, and all the names were "baby." *O.K., Susie,* I thought to myself, *this is war.*

I met Emily outside the mess hall. Already a war idea was brewing, but I kept still about it.

"Special lunch today," Emily greeted me.

"Oh, yeah?" I said suspiciously.

"Really," said Em. "We only get this four times a summer."

"What is it?" I asked. Emily really likes fruit salad and yogurt, so I wasn't sure whether I could trust her.

"Do-it-yourself hoagies and do-it-yourself sundaes."

"Wow! You're kidding," I cried.

The tables in the mess hall had been rearranged into two long buffet tables. Across one was spread every imaginable kind of sandwich filling and spread, from roast beef and ham to peanut butter and jelly. The other table wasn't finished, but it looked pretty promising. I saw marshmallow topping, whipped topping, strawberries, nuts, cherries, chocolate syrup, butterscotch, and big dishes to hold everything.

Emily and I walked beside the hoagie table, taking practically everything. Except anchovies. I felt sorry for the little anchovies. They weren't going to have too many takers.

We carried our hoagies out to the lawn where one week ago Dad and I had sat trying to picnic next to the

Fat Family. I couldn't believe it was just last week. It seemed like forever ago. It seemed unreal. Then, *hey!* I thought suddenly, *I've made it through half of Kate's trial period.* It hadn't all been good, but I'd made it!

Emily and I found Jan and Angela and Nancy, and we sat together in a bunch. It was the first meal we'd gotten to eat with our bunkies. I sat feeling glowy and contented, like a cat napping in a pool of sunshine.

When I saw Mary and Susie walk out of the mess hall with their hoagies and start to come over to us but turn away, my mood was spoiled, but only momentarily.

About half an hour later, after our incredibly large sundaes had disappeared and we were basking in the sun, lazy and drowsy, a shadow fell across my eyes. I opened them.

Mrs. Wright towered over me.

What now? I thought, panicked. *This time I really haven't done anything. I'm even willing to admit I'm having fun.*

"Kammy?" said Mrs. Wright lightly. She didn't sound angry, but she sounded the way Dad sounded the night he had to ask me whether the disappearance of the cookie jar money had anything to do with me. Like he was walking on eggshells.

"Yes?" I answered warily.

"I'm sorry to interrupt you, but I'd like to see you for a few minutes. . . . Don't worry. It's just for a chat." She smiled.

I looked at that smile very carefully. Sometimes you can see things hidden behind people's smiles. Dad says some of those things are called ulterior motives. He says I'll understand that term better when I get to be an adult.

Well, I didn't see anything else—like fury—behind

that smile, so I gave her back a wobbly little smile of my own and started to get up.

"Oh, you can wait until lunch is over," said Mrs. Wright. "Relax for a few more minutes. Then come along to my office."

There were about ten minutes before the gong would go off, but I couldn't enjoy them. Darn old Mrs. Wright.

What did she want me for, anyway? Maybe Susie was telling stories about me now. I wouldn't put it past her. To be frank, I wouldn't blame her.

Or maybe she had found out I got out of serving dinner last night by bribing Amanda Jacobs, who sat next to me.

I headed over to the office with sweaty palms and cold feet.

"Come in," Mrs. Wright called, as I knocked on the door.

I plopped myself down in the hard-backed chair opposite her desk. It felt like it was designed to support people without spines. Or to keep pilgrims awake in church.

Mrs. Wright tapped a pen nervously against a little paper-clip dish on her desk. "I know you're wondering why I called you in, and I hope I didn't embarrass you in front of your friends."

She paused.

I didn't say anything. Some remarks are best left unanswered.

"Well," she sighed, "I just wanted to talk to you. I feel I haven't been very fair to you. I didn't give you a chance to defend yourself the other night after the horror-story incident. Also, I feel we haven't honestly discussed whatever problems you may be having. I know you have not yet been completely honest about why you're doing the things you're doing. So now I want your side of all this. We've both had time to cool off since Thursday.

"I'm not letting you leave until I hear *everything*," she added. "It shouldn't matter to you much. You're only missing swimming." She gave me a sly look.

I ignored the sly look.

"Well?" she said.

"O.K.," I said.

"Let's start at the beginning. Why did you skip lunch on Tuesday?"

I took a deep breath. I felt cornered. I was also beginning to feel that Mrs. Wright was a bit dim. Maybe I should clue her in on the fact that she was running her camp all wrong. So I started talking.

And talking. And talking. And talking.

I told her about everything. From her long-distance bathrooms to her lack of privacy to her stupid serving arrangements.

"Well," said Mrs. Wright when I'd finished.

"Well," I said. "Do you have to take serious action now?"

"I don't think so," she said. The corners of her mouth twitched like she was trying to hide a smile.

"But we have to do something about these . . . these difficulties. First of all, let me point out that you've made all these—"

"Difficulties?" I supplied.

She cleared her throat. "Yes. You've made them worse by not telling me the truth before. If you had just told me—"

"But I didn't want to look like a baby!" I cried. "I'm *not* a baby."

"You don't *want* to be, but maybe deep down you're afraid you are."

I turned that thought over in my head while Mrs. Wright went on. "Anyway, now that it's all out in the open, we can do something."

I frowned at her. "Like what?"

"Well, for one thing, you're absolutely right. Girls your age need their privacy . . ."

My mouth dropped open. I couldn't believe it.

Mrs. Wright went on about solutions and things for fifteen more minutes or so. Let me tell you, when that conference was over, camp looked a whole lot brighter.

Mrs. Wright said she'd look into rigging up some kind of dressing room in every cabin. Then she said if serving bugged me so much, Amanda and I could be co-servers, and Amanda could take care of the parts I was worried about. And *then*, she assured me no one had ever spotted a snake in or near the lake, but since I was already a good swimmer there was no need for me to take lessons and I could spend every other lesson in the arts and crafts cabin, if I spent the in-between ones helping Marcia out (onshore, of course), doing things like keeping track of towels and organizing the Lower Girls for relay races.

I began twitching around in my seat, anxious to leave. Swimming lessons weren't over yet and I wanted to run right over to Sunny Skies for a while.

"One more thing, Kammy," Mrs. Wright said, looking stern. "You've got a few more nights to go in the kitchen. You're still on punishment for that incident with Susie. I know the two of you don't get along very well, but could you please make an effort with her? You don't really want to spend all your evenings washing dishes, do you?"

"No," I said hastily. "No. I promise I'll be nicer. I'm going to try real hard. Honestly."

"O.K.," said Mrs. Wright. She smiled warmly.

I dashed out of the office and practically flew to Sunny Skies to work on my quilt.

For the next few days everything went pretty well. Except for working in the kitchen. And Susie, of course.

I tried to ignore her, but she made that very difficult. She would stare at me during every meal and laugh if I did the slightest thing wrong.

She teased me as I headed into the kitchen after supper each night, giggling with Mary and pointing at me and telling anyone who would listen how I had run away from lunch and cried and been in trouble with Mrs. Wright and had to wash dishes.

I thought when you ignored somebody he or she was supposed to lose interest in you. But the more I ignored Susie, the more she followed me around, laughing at me and informing me I was a baby.

I was growing angrier and angrier at her. There were times when I wanted to grab her and throw her across the cabin. But I learned to keep my feelings inside.

In between, I was actually having fun.

With all the extra time I was putting in at Sunny Skies, Baby Boy's quilt was really coming along. I was making it out of patches of yellow checks, blue checks, yellow flowers, and blue flowers. It took several hours to do each row. I was working slowly and carefully and not making any mistakes.

One day (it was Tuesday, as a matter of fact; I remember because for some reason Susie was in the class that day, which spoiled it just a little for me), Janine held up my quilt for all the other girls to see. She explained the pattern I was using and said the stitching was good and wanted to know where I learned it.

I grinned so wide it was hard to talk. As I told everyone about quilting, a bunch of girls (not Susie) crowded around. They asked questions and said the quilt was pretty. I practically burst.

After class, I ran all the way to the mess hall and told Amanda I thought I could handle serving by myself.

Which I did.

That night the Upper Girls had a treasure hunt. The counselors had hidden these funny riddles all over camp. Guess who cracked the final one which led to the treasure? And guess what the treasure was—a gigantic piñata filled with gum drops and jawbreakers, Tootsie Rolls and sour balls, root beer barrels and licorice sticks and barley bears. It was terrific! We spent the evening trading for favorites.

That second week was getting to be one good day after another. I looked forward to arts and crafts and horseback riding and didn't have to worry about the lake.

A couple of evenings we had meetings to work on the Visiting Day skit. We always started off the meetings by going into the woods and doing our special exercises. I was used to it by now. Also, the scenery was coming along fine and I had memorized my two grandmother lines.

Then came Thursday.

During Siesta I got a letter from Dad.

He started out with the usual news. Simon was going through a pouncing stage. At the university, classes were under way and teaching was a hot profession in the summer, ha ha. And for some reason, Kate didn't like Hercules or Sherlock as names for Baby Boy. Dad sounded very put out.

Then he got down to what he apparently considered the most important part of the letter, since he spent close to three pages on it. Muffin's birthday party. It had been held last Saturday. The way Dad went on about it, you'd have thought it was his own party.

I tried to skip over this part of the letter, but it meant skipping from almost the very beginning to the very end. Besides, if you've ever tried *not* to read part of anything anyone has handwritten to you personally, you know it is next to impossible. So I waded through the whole grisly description.

How Dad had had fun (he even had the nerve to say he felt like a little boy again) helping Muffin and her infant friends play musical chairs and pin-the-tail-on-the-donkey. (Considering he'd never done that for me, I was surprised he knew how.)

How they'd ordered this gigantic pink cake from the Village Bakery. (I wondered what Mrs. Meade thought of that. She always *made* my birthday cakes. Dad said ordering from the bakery was extravagant.)

How Dad and Kate and Muffin had gone to the Hunt Brothers' Circus that night where (once again) Dad felt like a little boy, and Muffin was chosen out of the audience to ride an elephant at the show's finale.

I hoped Muffin cried. I hoped she hated it.

This was the end of Dad's letter:

> Well, sweetheart, we'll see you on Saturday.
> We're all coming up. Except Simon, of course.
> He has asked to stay home so he can watch TV.

I almost laughed at that, but managed to hold back.

> I hope camp is better and you are enjoying
> yourself.
>> Lots of love and hugs and kisses,
>>> Your Old Dad

Well. He had certainly left out something important. He hadn't forgotten the deal about how I could come home on Saturday if I wanted, had he? I mean, that *was* the agreement, right? I wasn't hallucinating.

Somewhere deep inside me I could feel fear nagging. Not much. Just a little. But I began to worry. What if they didn't plan on keeping their promise? They wouldn't do that, would they?

I didn't think so. I would hope for the best. That was all I could do. Just hope.

CHAPTER 12

War on Susie

I was still brooding over Visiting Day when I remembered that today was a Sunny Skies day. I jogged over there after Siesta, mentally planning the next row of Baby Boy's quilt. It was a center row, one of the most important. I wanted it to be perfect.

I let myself into the cabin and flicked on the lights. Sometimes Janine was there and sometimes she wasn't. Today she wasn't.

In a cupboard were all my carefully cut out squares and triangles of fabric. I already knew just which ones I'd need, so I took them out and laid them down on a table. Then I went to another cupboard to get the box the partially finished quilt was kept in. I carried it carefully over to the table, lifted the lid—and stared in horror.

The quilt was shredded.

It lay in its box in ragged strips and pieces. You couldn't even tell it was supposed to have been a quilt. Holding back hot tears, I stared at it for a few more seconds, then shoved the lid back on the box and threw the whole thing on the floor. I kicked it savagely, left it under a bench, and swept the new squares off the table, watching them flutter to the floor. It didn't even occur to me to wonder who did it. I just couldn't believe the

quilt was ruined. I had wanted so much to give it to Kate
and make her proud of me.

I swiped at the light switch until the room dimmed,
banged out of Sunny Skies, and ran to our cabin.

Nancy was there reading a book called *Forbidden Love*.
It was her afternoon off.

I burst through her curtain, sobbing.

It took a while, but I was finally able, in between a lot
of gulping and hiccupping, to tell her what I had discov-
ered.

She took me by the hand and we walked over to Sunny
Skies for another look.

Sure enough.

There wasn't really anything to do. Or say.

We just went back to Misty Mountains, where I lay
down on my bunk feeling sort of ill. Nancy dug up a can
of Coke from somewhere for me, and lent me her copy
of *The Hobbit*. Even with all my disappointment and
anger, I found it in me to ask her if I could borrow
Forbidden Love instead. We both laughed and felt better.

Then Nancy climbed up to sit on my bunk with me
and said, "I know it's trite, but it *is* true that you can start
another quilt. I remember when my puppy, Mocha, was
killed. Everyone said, 'You can get another puppy,' and
I hated them for it. But soon I did get another one.
Popeye. And I loved him just as much as Mocha. Not in
the same way, but just as much."

"Yeah," I said tonelessly. "I think maybe what I'll do
is forget about the quilt for a while."

"That's probably a very good idea."

"You know what would make me feel a lot better?" I
asked.

"What?"

"If I found the person who did that and hit her so hard she landed in Arizona."

Nancy laughed again, but then she said seriously, "Kammy, I know you're strong-willed, and I also know you have a strong sense of fairness. I'm sure you'd like a little revenge. But if we should find out who destroyed your quilt, would you please take it easy? Leave the punishing up to Mrs. Wright?"

"O.K.," I said uncertainly. I wasn't sure I could do that.

About ten minutes later all my bunkies came yelping and leaping back into the cabin. Swimming lessons were over.

They crowded around me wanting to know if I was sick or something.

Susie appeared, too, and I steeled myself for a real barrage of teasing and singing. But instead she said sweetly, "Oh, I'm *so* sorry about your quilt."

Well, that brought me up short because I hadn't *told* any of the girls about the quilt yet. I had only just started to explain that no, I wasn't sick, and no, I had not gotten my period for the first time.

So I said, just as sweetly, "Why, thank you, Susie," and went on to explain to the others about Baby Boy's poor quilt.

After swimming, we had free time until supper, so as soon as I could, I grabbed Emily and took her aside. "I've got to talk to you," I whispered urgently.

"Meet me at the amph in fifteen minutes," she said.

The amph was the amphitheater, our small outdoor theater set on a little rise behind the boathouse. It was on the edge of the campgrounds and we didn't use it much. It was a quiet, private place, perfect for war plans.

"Going swimming," Emily yelled to Nancy as she dashed out the door.

"Going for a walk," I yelled a few minutes later.

We met up at the amph. Emily was sprawled along a bench chewing gum.

"You won't believe this," I said angrily as I plopped down next to her. "Guess who ruined my quilt."

Emily opened her eyes wide. "Who?"

"Susie."

"Come on, Kammy. You're kidding. I know she has it in for you, but—"

"No. It's true," I interrupted her. "Susie said something about being sorry to hear about my quilt—before I told anyone, except Nancy."

"Gosh," said Emily slowly.

"Yeah," I said. "And now she's had it. She's really had it. She's been mean to me all week, I ignored her, and look what she did anyway. I promised Nancy I wouldn't take revenge on her, but I'm going to have to. This is war. So listen to this plan. We are going to give her exactly what she wants—and exactly what she deserves."

"Kammy, I don't know . . ."

"Just listen, O.K.?" I said. "It's sort of funny. It won't actually hurt her. And if you don't want to be in on it, you don't have to be."

"All right."

"It's very simple. We just issue, in secret, an anonymous invitation to each girl in our cabin to come to a private party tomorrow night. We say the invitations are only for a select few of the coolest girls at camp, and not to talk about the party. The invitations will say to sneak down to Lake Oconomowoc and to bring any goodies that can be raided from the kitchen. The only thing is, all the invitations will say to come at midnight. Except Susie's. Her time will be eleven forty-five, which will give me just enough time to scare the pants off her with a reenactment of 'Three-Fingered Willie.' Susie'll look like a real fool by the time the other girls arrive for the 'party.' "

Emily grinned. "It would be kind of funny."

"*Will* be, Em," I said. "Will be."

"Ooooosuuuuu. Suseeeee," Emily began to howl.

I giggled.

"But how do you know Susie will go along with this? What if she doesn't pay attention to her invitation? She'll have to break rules—" Emily said.

"Don't worry. She'll do it. She's dying to be part of anything here at camp. Nobody likes her and she knows it. But to think she's considered one of the coolest girls at camp. She'll fall all over herself."

"All we have to do is make four invitations, give them out in secret, and make sure Susie gets the different one."

"When do we start?" asked Em.

"As soon as we get to some paper and pencils."

Friday night. Ten-thirty.

My mind was in a whirl. In a little over an hour Emily and I would pull off a stunt to top all stunts. Just the thought of the quilt was enough to make me want to rip Susie's teeth out. One by one. No Novocaine.

I hadn't been within a hundred yards of Sunny Skies all day.

Tomorrow was on my mind, too.

Dad! Would he really let me come home if I wanted to?

I couldn't wait to see him. I decided I wouldn't even mind seeing Kate and Muffin and Baby Boy.

Funny. I still didn't know what decision I was going to make about camp. Camp was fun now. I was tempted to stay. On the other hand, without me around, Muffin was getting an awful lot of attention from Dad. On the third hand, I bet she still cried and puked, and had Baby Boy licked his colic yet? On the fourth hand, Kate was going to teach me stuff and . . .

The time ticked by.

Eleven o'clock. All systems go. Invitations issued, and probably found. A lot of odd, furtive looks during dinner, and a ridiculous amount of smirking on Susie's part.

Eleven-forty. Susie snuck out of the cabin.

Eleven forty-five. I snuck out of the cabin.

By now I knew my way around camp in the dark as well as anyone else. My feet flew along paths, over roots and stones, through the woods to Lake Oconomowoc. Without the aid of a flashlight. When I reached the edge of the woods I stopped for a moment. The moon was full and lit up the lake like a football stadium at night.

I scanned the shore for Susie.

Sure enough, there she was, standing uncertainly at the edge of the lake.

I watched her for a few seconds.

Even though we were both alone, Susie looked somehow more alone than I felt.

I was about to begin howling when something suddenly came over me. To this day I don't know exactly what it was.

"Susie!" I called, and ran across the sand to her.

She eyed me suspiciously.

"Susie, it's a joke," I said.

"What?"

"It's a joke. I just wanted to get you down here and scare you. I was going to make you think Three-Fingered Willie was after you. The other girls are coming in a few minutes for a party. They would have caught you down here screaming about that stupid horror story again. I wanted to get back at you. . . . I know you ruined the quilt."

Susie just stared. She didn't say anything for a long time. In the moonlight, I could see her eyes bright with tears. She was gulping furiously. Finally she managed to squeak out, "How did you know?"

"It doesn't matter," I said. "I just figured it out. But I didn't tell anyone except Emily. I'm not going to tell Nancy. And the other girls don't know the party is a joke on you. They think it's a real party." I paused. "Would you please tell me why you did that to my quilt? I worked so hard on it." Now I was close to tears myself. "I wanted to give it to my stepmother. It was for my little stepbrother. I was trying to show Kate—oh, shoot, I don't know." I had to stop talking before I started crying, too. "But why did you?" I demanded fiercely.

"Because," Susie blurted out, "you were so mean to me. Everyone's mean to me. And because you came here, a new kid at camp, and everyone liked you. Emily, Nancy, Angela, everyone. Even though you had all these problems and caused trouble. They liked you anyway. And I've been here forever, and I do everything right and don't cause any trouble, and I still don't have any friends. Except Mary. And she would have made friends with a warthog if one had smiled at her the first day of camp."

We both laughed uneasily.

"Then that day in art class—when Janine showed off your quilt?"

I nodded.

"It was just too much. All that attention. I was so mad at you. And you *had* played those tricks on me."

I nodded again.

"Now will you tell me something?" Susie asked. Her voice sounded normal again. "How come you're getting me out of this?"

"I don't know," I said slowly. "I just couldn't go through with it. It was too mean, I guess. Even if you did ruin all the work I put into that quilt. I know it would have scared you to death."

Through the trees we could hear hushed whispers and little crunchings and cracklings.

"Here come the others," I said. "Don't worry. I won't tell them. And I'll explain everything to Emily later. But you owe me, Susie."

"What?"

"You owe me one. I got you out of this, so now promise something. Promise you'll quit bugging me, O.K.?"

"That's all?"

"Yes."

"All *right!*" she cried.

We grinned at each other.

CHAPTER 13

Starting Over

Well, Susie and I didn't become overnight buddies or anything after that night, but we did make an effort either to avoid each other or to be civil. Sometimes we even tried being nice, which actually was not all that bad.

What happened after I rescued Susie was that the other four girls came crashing out of the woods. (I decided that at some future date I'd have to show them how to sneak properly.) Anyway, they were delighted to find Susie and me by the lake.

"Oh, it's a Misty Mountains party!" cried Mary with more enthusiasm than I'd heard since the morning Sunny Skies opened. I guess, like Susie, she was pretty glad to be part of anything, even if it was just her own cabin—which she was already part of, but I didn't bother to point that out to her.

While everyone was standing around debating the pros and cons of going for a dip in the lake at that hour (there were a lot more cons than pros), Emily grabbed me by the sleeve of my GREAT ADVENTURE T-shirt and pulled me away from the group.

"What's going on?" she demanded.

"Oh, calm down," I said crossly. "What's going on is nothing. I couldn't go through with it. I decided it was

139

too mean a trick to play. So I came down here early and had a little talk with Susie. You'll be delighted to know she won't be bugging us—well, me, anyway—anymore. But I did promise her something before she promised that back."

"What?"

"That you and I would keep our mouths shut about this whole thing—the quilt, Three-Fingered Willie, everything. O.K.?"

Emily shrugged.

"Come on," I said. "I promised. And she'll be out of our hair. That's worth something, isn't it?"

"Yeah," Emily said at last. She heaved a great sigh. "I was all set for a little excitement."

"It'll be pretty exciting if we make it back into our bunks without waking up Nancy. Anyway, Jan and Angela and Mary are expecting a party. Remember? Let's get the food."

I walked over to the beachhouse and returned with a large bag of marshmallows I had relieved the kitchen of earlier. I also had a book of matches.

The girls had decided it was too cold to go swimming, so I handed the matches over to Susie, who built a perfect fire in record time. We toasted the marshmallows, roasted hot dogs (from Emily), stuffed ourselves with brownies and cookies and soda (from the other girls), and told ghost stories very, very quietly.

The six of us sat around for over an hour and didn't want to leave, but we figured it might cause a stir if Nancy came to and found her entire cabin missing, so we finally put out the fire and crept back to Misty Mountains. I think Nancy did wake up as we were all getting settled, but she didn't say anything. Which was very nice of her.

I slept so well that night, I woke up later than usual the next morning and just barely got myself dressed before reveille.

It was Saturday morning!

Saturday at last.

Dad, Kate, Muffin and Baby Boy arrived a little after eleven.

All us campers were hanging out on the main lawn near the mess hall watching the stream of visitors pour off the little path from the parking lot.

I saw Dad first. He was carrying Muffin on his shoulders. The way he used to carry me. Kate was behind him with Baby Boy and the diaper bag.

I waved tentatively at Dad, but just at that second he looked up at Muffin, laughed, and tugged on her sandals.

I tried again.

Suddenly he saw me. His face lit up with a huge grin. He swung Muffin down, led her back to Kate, and ran to me.

I couldn't stand it. I jumped up and ran to him, too. We crashed into each other. I grabbed him around the waist and clung to him.

Then, to my surprise, as much as to Dad's, I started crying, and I sobbed until his shirt was all wet, with a big patch that was a darker yellow than the rest. He didn't ask me any questions or tell me not to cry. He just held me and patted my back until I pulled away and looked up at him. I smiled sheepishly.

Muffin and Kate had caught up with us, and Muffin,

looking more adorable than ever in a frilly little sundress and red sandals, smiled hugely at me.

"Hi," I said.

"I don't have Rose-up with me," she said.

Now, a couple of weeks ago that comment might have really thrown me, but I was getting used to little kids.

"My goodness," I said seriously. "Where is she?"

"At home. On my bed." Muffin crossed her arms and sighed heavily.

"Is that where she stays now?"

"Yup."

"I bet you can do that because you're four years old, right?"

"Yes!" Muffin managed to look surprised and pleased and proud all at once.

I caught Dad and Kate exchanging happy glances.

"Well, I think that's terrific," I told Muffin. And I meant it.

Then I realized I hadn't greeted Kate.

I stepped over to her.

"Hi, Kate."

Kate handed Baby Boy over to Dad.

"Hi, honey," she said.

Before I knew it I had reached out and given her an awkward little hug around the waist. She kissed my forehead. Neither of us said anything.

When all the sloppy stuff was over, I suddenly realized I had a lot to show everybody.

"Come on!" I said. "We have an hour until lunch. You have to see the horses. And Sunny Skies!"

I dragged them all over camp. I showed them the lake and the art stuff and the horses and the amph. Muffin especially liked the horses. Sharon was at Haven, and she lifted Muffin onto Mr. Chips, and I led them around the ring a couple of times. Muffin was ecstatic. When she got off, Sharon let me demonstrate my jumping. Muffin was so impressed it was embarrassing.

"I want to do that someday," she kept saying. "Just like you. Just like you, Kammy."

I took them to Misty Mountains next. I had a surprise there for Muffin.

"This is my bunk," I said as we entered the cabin, "and this is Nancy's room, and this is where I keep my trunk." I opened it. Muffin peered inside curiously. I guess she'd already forgotten how she watched Kate and Mrs. Meade pack it for a week.

"I think there's something in here for you, Muffin," I said, like I had just remembered it.

"There *is?*" she asked, wide-eyed.

"Mm-hmm." I reached in and pulled out a little box. Emily had lent me the box just for this occasion. She kept her earrings in it. "It's a birthday present," I said. "I'm sorry I couldn't get it to you on your real birthday, but I made it and it wasn't finished on time."

"Did you make it at Sunny Skies?" she asked.

"Yes," I said, completely bowled over that she'd think of that. Four-year-old minds can be very hard to figure out.

Muffin lifted the lid on the box and stared. I couldn't tell if she was happy or if she didn't know what the present was.

"They're barrettes," I filled her in. "For your hair."

I had taken two of my own barrettes and glued tiny beads and seashells on them.

"Ooh," breathed Muffin. "Mommy, can we put them on?"

"Sure," replied Kate.

I fixed them in Muffin's hair and she looked pleased as punch. She even remembered to thank me.

After that it was time to go back to the mess hall for lunch. Actually, we ate on the main lawn in front of the mess hall, where another picnic was spread out. I ate a whole lot more this time than I did two weeks ago.

It was at some point during lunch that Muffin started to get fussy.

First she refused to eat the potato salad because it had black specks in it. Kate kept telling her they were just pepper, but it didn't seem to matter to Muffin. (I couldn't blame her. I wasn't eating the potato salad for the same reason.)

Then Muffin wouldn't finish her milk because she said it tasted funny. Dad pointed out to her that she didn't seem to mind the taste of the half she'd already drunk, but Muffin wouldn't give an inch.

(Along about now Baby Boy began to cry. I wondered how his colic was getting along, but I was afraid to ask.)

I tried to ignore everything and enjoy the picnic, but it was tough.

As Dad was telling me how Simon had come within inches of catching a small spider, Emily wandered over. Her parents weren't at camp. They lived so far away they only came to one Visiting Day each summer. Emily didn't mind.

"Hi," she said, standing by our little group. She sounded almost shy.

"Hi!" I answered happily. "Everybody, this is Emily. She's my bunkie."

Dad stood up and shook her hand politely. He invited her to sit down with us.

Emily sat.

Kate smiled and said, "Glad to meet you."

Muffin pouted, for some reason I'll never figure out.

And Baby Boy let loose one of his louder squawks.

Emily looked slightly alarmed.

"You'll have to forgive him," Kate apologized. "I think he's sleepy."

Why he couldn't just drop off was beyond me.

Emily noticed the barrettes in Muffin's hair and asked her how she liked them. Muffin stared at her sandals.

"Oh, that reminds me," I said suddenly, ignoring Muffin's lack of manners. "Do you have the box the barrettes came in, Muffin? It belongs to Emily."

Muffin looked at me warily.

"Do you have the box?" I asked again.

Muffin nodded.

"Can you please give it to Emily? It's hers." I was being as patient as I knew how.

"No," said Muffin.

"No?"

"It's mine."

"No," I said very carefully. My father once told me my voice gets an "edge" to it when I'm angry. I carefully kept the edge out of my voice. "The barrettes are yours," I explained, "but Emily *lent* us the box they came in. Now we have to give it back to her."

Well, that did it.

Muffin turned on the tears.

She and Baby Boy were both crying to beat the band. I took a casual look around to see how much of a scene we were creating. Several people were staring, but that seemed to be about it.

After a few minutes of pleading and explaining, we got the box back from Muffin and I handed it to Emily, who had turned a fierce shade of red and kept repeating she didn't really *need* the box; she could keep her earrings in her soap dish.

It was taking a great deal of effort on my part not to blow up. I felt quite explosive.

Luckily, the gong sounded before anything too awful happened. All picnickers fell quiet, Muffin included. Kate stuck a teething ring in Baby Boy's mouth, and that silenced him for a while.

Mrs. Wright stood up and announced that the girls of Camp Arrowhead were going to present a program for Visiting Day.

We had had a meeting about this over a week ago and we all knew what would happen. Just about every camper was in the program. The Lower Girls would present their stuff first. Emily and I could watch until intermission, when we'd have to get ready for our parts. I was going to be in the drama group play. Emily was in a group that was going to do choral speaking, whatever that was.

Mostly what the Lower Girls did was sing. The littlest ones charmed us with an off-key rendition of "B-I-N-G-O," the next oldest ones sang "My Grandfather's Clock" with a lot of sound effects and gestures, and the oldest ones performed "So Long, Farewell" from *The Sound of Music.* Last of all, a special group put on a play,

The Three Bears. It was really cute. The girls playing bears were wearing bear ears and bear noses and bear paws and bear tails. When they first came on, I looked over at Muffin to see how she was enjoying it. She was sound asleep.

Intermission came and I asked Dad if maybe he or Kate could wake Muffin up just enough so she could see me as the grandmother in our play, *Flabby Tabby and the Blue Balloon Mystery.*

Dad said they'd see.

After that came a flurry of getting ready. *Flabby Tabby* was the closing performance. While the other groups did their thing, Angela, Cassandra, me, and the rest of our group ran around getting our costumes together, putting on makeup, setting up the scenery, and finding the props.

All I had to do in the play was walk onto the set during the second act, let my glasses fall off, say, "Oh, my," wait for Inspector Gardell to pick them up for me, and say, "Thank you, sir." It may not sound like much, but it was crucial to the mystery, because when Inspector Gardell picks up the glasses he sees that the grandmother wears trifocals and therefore could not *possibly* have been the mysterious figure without glasses seen shooting BBs at blue balloons the week before.

Our group had gotten itself all ready by the time Emily's choral speaking performance began. It turned out that choral speaking meant a group of people reciting something together. It was like a choir talking instead of singing. They recited the poem "Wynken, Blynken, and Nod," with different groups saying each stanza.

It sounded really neat and I was trying to enjoy it, but I couldn't concentrate. Suddenly I noticed my stomach didn't feel so hot. I looked around for Cassandra.

"Cassandra?" I said when I found her. I was feeling pretty sick by then, and I guess my voice was sort of shaking, because right away Cassandra said, "Oh, no, not you, too."

She led me to a shady spot where three pale girls from our group were sitting. One of them was Angela. She was holding a plastic bag in case she barfed.

"What is it?" I gasped. "Food poisoning?"

"No, silly," said Cassandra, but she said it in a caring way, not a mean way. "It's called butterflies. You've all got a good case of stage fright. You've got to get your minds off the play."

"If I do that," wailed Angela, "I'll forget my lines."

"No, you won't," Cassandra promised. "We've rehearsed so much, they'll come to you just like that"—she snapped her fingers—"as soon as we get going. Now I want you to try something. Have you ever played Concentration?"

Cassandra started teaching us the crazy complicated circle game with hand-clapping and finger-snapping. It took a lot of *concentration*. Anyway, we got so carried away trying to keep it going, we started giggling and forgot about our stomachs. Angela even got rid of the plastic bag.

Before we knew it, "Wynken, Blynken, and Nod" was over and Cassandra was waving us back to the group. We had no time to worry about anything. The play began.

I guess it must have looked a little funny. I mean, we weren't using the amph or anything because our audience was too big, and we didn't have a real stage, just my scenery all propped up on the lawn in front of the mess hall; but it didn't seem to matter.

The first act went off with only one small hitch. Bonita Evans, who was cast as the Flabby Tabby, tripped over her flabby tabby tail and almost killed Inspector Gardell. Otherwise, everything went fine. I hoped Dad liked my scenery.

Act II began, and I stood behind the scenery waiting to make my grandmother entrance. Me. Kamilla Whitlock. I had never done anything like this before.

I listened for my cue, and when I heard it, walked right on the stage (I think you could even say I walked on with confidence), let my glasses slip off, said, "Oh, my," and "Thank you, sir," at just the right places, and walked calmly offstage.

Then I hugged Cassandra, who understood.

The play ended and everyone in our group, including Cassandra, joined hands and walked in front of the scenery in a line. We took a bow, and our audience applauded. I frantically searched the sea of faces for Dad's. And for Kate's and Muffin's. I was sure I'd never find them. But I did!

Lo and behold, Muffin was awake. She was waving at me and smiling again. Maybe she just needed a little nap to get over being fussy. After all, she *was* just four years old. I grinned at her.

A few minutes later, everything was over and I was back with my family.

"Well," said Dad, "it's time to make a decision."

"I know," I said.

Dad looked at me very seriously. He reached out and

touched my cheek. "It's completely up to you. . . . Are you leaving or staying?"

I looked back at him. I couldn't read anything on his face—except kindness. I thought I might find a hint there, like whether he *wanted* me to stay. But no hint.

I checked Kate. No hint there either.

"O.K.," I said at last. "I'm leaving with you."

Dad smiled. "All right, sweetie. And Kate and I want you to know we're very proud of you. You tried something you were scared of and you stuck it out. Not many people would do that."

"Oh, Kammy," said Kate. "I'm glad you're coming home. I know you and I got off to a bad start, but I've missed you these two weeks! I'm glad we don't have to wait six more before we start over."

Well, that was more than I had hoped to hear. I swallowed quickly a couple of times. I had something important to say.

"Wait a minute," I said. "Wait. I'm not coming home. I'm—I'm staying here. I have things to finish," I said, thinking of Baby Boy's quilt. "And—and Emily's going to be here six more weeks. I can't desert her. And our drama group's going to put on some more plays, and I'm going to be in a horse show and everything. And we can write letters. And, Kate, in six more weeks maybe you can get the house all organized and clear up the baby's colic and—"

"Kammy," she stopped me, putting her hand on my arm, "It's O.K. I understand."

I think she really did.

We all hung around for a little while longer, and then the visitors began to drift off.

Dad looked at his watch. "I think we'd better get a

move on," he said. "Simon will be wanting us to serve his dinner."

"Oh, *Dad*," I groaned.

We all stood up.

Dad lifted Muffin onto his shoulders. "Remember when I used to carry you this way?" he asked me.

"Yeah," I said wistfully.

"Somehow you seemed a lot lighter."

"That's because you were a lot younger."

"Oh, *Kammy*," he groaned.

I picked up the diaper bag, and we walked to the car. We got the kids and the bag loaded in, and I kissed Dad and Kate good-bye.

Dad had just started pulling out of his parking space when I thought of something. "Hey!" I cried. "I know what to name the baby!"

The car stopped. Dad and Kate poked their heads out of the front windows.

"What?" my father asked.

"Call him Robert, after you, Dad."

Dad and Kate turned to each other and smiled. Then Kate flashed me the thumbs-up sign out the window, and Dad said, "I love you, Kams."

They started to drive off again and then jerked to another stop as Kate poked her head back out the window.

"Kammy," she called, "we have to start planning a party. You'll have your birthday right after you come home from camp in August."

"A party?" I echoed. "For me?"

"Of course!" cried Kate. "What's a birthday without a party?"

This time they drove off for real.

Muffin and I waved until the car turned a corner and we couldn't see each other anymore.

I headed back to Misty Mountains to find my bunkies. I had news for them.

About the Author

Ann M. Martin grew up in Princeton, New Jersey, and was graduated from Smith College. She has a passion for roller skating, mysteries, and cats.

Bummer Summer is her first novel. Her second novel, *Inside Out*, is also available as an Apple Paperback.

Ann Martin lives in New York City, where she is a full-time writer.